Refuel your Imagination
The world may be stifling true creativity, but that's no reason to let yourself go. Keep your imagination fit with thrilling and almond-activating stories from Aegeon.

Science Fiction
Aegeon
Illustrated

Aegeon Issue Number 3: October, 2022

www.aegeon-scifi.com

Editor-in-chief: Brendan Heard
Assistant Editors: Alice Ilona, Rick Damer
Advertising Manager: Hermann Zoltaz

Cover art (from Eternal Life) by AMH
Interior illustrations by Brendan Heard except for:
Max Ryan & page 75 Ramek by Erwin Reuss
Perambulator Lich and Apnea designs by AMH
Map of Heaven by Michael Gallo
Parables of the Biomancer by William Watts @veelhell
Psychic Assassin & Patriarch by Artist of Albion t.me/artistofalbion
King's Blood by Mark Straker (author)

ISBN: 9798355310394
Original printing by Amazon KDP. Published by The Aureus Press.

www.aureus-press.com.

The Aureus Press is a publisher of fiction and non-fiction on the topics of imagination, history, art, technology and culture.

Ramek feels a sensation upon witnessing your return to the pages of Aegeon, pre-livestock terrans. It is a sensation similar to a warm and suspiciously weak nostalgia, which frankly sickens Ramek with its potentially perilous sentimental frailty.

Nevertheless, here you are.

Yet there is a kind of victory in your return from which Ramek will allow himself a fleeting alleviation. It is as though an old friend has returned from the field, their arms melted off by machine thaser-cannons, bleeding from arcworm bites, their filthy face streaked with tears to see his old friend Ramek guarding the threshold of the battle-warren.

Ramek wants you know he will permit this sensation, temporarily, for as long as it takes your primitive ocular system to imbibe this opening scribe. For the battle is hard, and the war is long, and we require all returning soldiers to have a haven, where old friends can congratulate and re-equip them for the next front.

For the war never ends, techno-slave, and every haven is but a waystop.

This issue has more published submissions than ever, with all being of high entertainment value. There are also more contributor illustrations than ever, including the first cover not designed by Mr. Heard, which has been painted by the mysterious female unit known as AMH.

Many other new talents appear in this issue, armed with unique stories, as well as returning serials. Ramek is very excited about the piece known as *Apnea* which struck him as quite prescient and convincing for what humans of your era are beginning to experience as a matter of daily routine. And what you can expect to experience much more of, until the technology illusion cracks, and the steel tentacles of the Dark-System-God unleashes pure mechanical thinking upon the blighted earth.

We have the returning serials of *The Onyx Horseman, I am Dreaming*, and *Patriarch*, as well as a new serial by the name of *King's Blood*, which is alarmingly similar to a historic fantasy tale, although I think the intuitive reader will glean it as ultimately a cosmic fiction. Naturally it doesn't matter overly - what are you going to do about it? To Ramek and the editor of Aegeon, science fiction needs strong elements of both history and fantasy, and these worlds cross each other very easily, and even more easily when cosmic fiction is the over-arching umbrella.

The ongoing Ferrand PI serial will return next issue. Remember that Ramek has seen your future, gunthlings. Not the fiery inferno future of war and enslavement, but the closer future. The one where you subscribe to the Aegeon newsletter, and do not miss an issue as they come out, and loyally support Aegeon by leaving Amazon reviews, and by recommending it to others.

By the horns of Unruled Thazak.

EDITORIAL
Mckenna's Universe

Terence McKenna said many interesting things. As a man of the era of high science fiction, when future possibilities were blossoming and the vistas seemed truly wide open (they still are, but are obscured by a present tyranny of limitations).

Aptly, Mckenna said that language is the battleground over which the fight will take place, because what we cannot say, we cannot communicate.

This seems very fitting in our current age of censorship and politically correct manipulation of language, which McKenna had noted and spoken out against shortly before he died in 2000.

McKenna also said that we can conceive of things that we cannot communicate. That the psychedelic inner astronaut sees things which no human being has seen before. The tragedy of this being that it has little value unless it is possible to carry it back and explain it to the collective.

"Now as you know, biology runs on genes. And genes are the units of meaning of heredity. But we could make a model of the informational environment that is represented by culture, and in fact this is done. A word has been invented — meme. A meme is not the smallest unit of heredity. A meme is the smallest unit of meaning of an idea.

"Ideas are made of memes, and I think the art community might function with more efficiency in the production of visionary aesthetic breakthroughs, if we would think of ourselves as an environment, modeled after the natural environment, where we as artists are attempting to create memes which enter an environment of other memes that are in competition with each other, and out of this competition of memes, evermore appropriate adapted and suitable ideas can gather and link themselves together into higher and higher organisms.

"Somehow we have to internalize the entirety of the biological world if we are going to become a spacefaring spe-

cies, otherwise we are going to get out there and discover that something vital was left behind."

A very interesting quote from Terrence, from the age before social media, and the prevalence and relevance of this term 'meme' today. McKenna saw history as an alchemical task and process, heading towards an ultimate biological or civilizational goal. He believed the artist, as artificer, was beholden to the alchemical task of melding the worlds of 'mind' and 'matter'. This is a goal we take seriously here at Aegeon, where future speculation, psychedelic experience, history, and evolution are common themes, and where the art of presenting memes and ideas is a paramount concern.

McKenna believed that we humans cannot conceive of a coincidentia-oppositorum (the coincidence of opposites). And yet that is what we must hold in our minds if we want to seek truth. That even in quantum physics we see that the universe is composed of islands of boolean algebra embedded in an ocean of ordinary algebra. Which points to an ultimate truth also suggested in the philosophy of Frank Herbert's Dune: that everything is relative and absolute at the same time. That we as humans cannot conceive of constructs which are not dual opposites, but can be two things, even opposites, at the same time. A notion I personally feel was better understood in classical thought. To quote Terrence in conclusion:

"And it is an irrational process. It isn't a Nietzschean program of realization. It's a kind of an opening. Something wants to be born. The prompting of our religions with all the irrational and hysterical trappings that attend them nevertheless have a core perception that there is between man and nature a kind of compact, and this compact is, it will be redeemed. I mean I really think that this is the psychedelic faith. That we are the prodigal species.

"We have descended into the inferno of matter to try and recover the pearl of immortality."

\- Ed

Perambulator Lich
By Buffalo Jenkins

Elfina cautiously walked down the asteroid catacombs.

She discarded the remnant tatters of her spacesuit, proceeding in her underwear, having long lost her helmet and pack. She was petit, and feline, and her long blonde hair spilled out of its braids, and she rubbed blood from a cut on her thigh with a dirty hand as she padded down the steps. She lit the way ahead of her with her flashlight.

Be sure to follow the map, Jimmy had told her. *But here I am, without a map, and all paths head down.*

The steps descended for what felt like forever. The walls were irregular in the sparse light, and she paused to shine the light directly upon them. They were lined with mummified humanoids of some type, and the foundations were also filled with skulls, stacked together like mortared bricks. Many were human, but not all. Some were gargantuan, possibly Moltard skulls. *Brought in as labourers when this was still a mine,* she thought.

She noted the mauve slime growing in some corners of the stonework. *Eelmoss,* she thought, one absent touch of that and she would slowly go insane from algaeic poison. She felt highly aware of her near-nakedness.

The catacombs had a constant downward curvature, like an unending spiral stair. In spots the wall would vanish on one side to reveal a vast and seemingly bottomless pit, vanishing into blackness, sometimes blowing with a rank wind. She knew the stair would circle downward until she reached a treasure-nest. What kind of ancient creature or booby-trap was waiting there for her, she could not guess. She just knew it had destroyed Elmer Redbeard's team, and the only message that Elmer managed to transmit before vanishing was what sounded like: 'Oh no! The Perambulator Lich!'

Without warning one of the human mummies came out of its wall-alcove and reached for her with a ghastly groan. Her blaster belt was still tied to her naked thigh, and she drew and fired a bright red plasma burst into the horrid thing. It exploded in dust and old bones, its ancient wrappings catching alight and illuminating the gloom. It was so bright in that moment that she caught a glimpse of motion much further down the stair, leaping briskly out of sight around the next bend. She could not make out what it was, but it was humanoid.

My life is full of jerks, trying to surprise me.

She put a hand to her mouth, choking on the foul dust, pointing her flashlight at the remains. Poking around with her boot, she saw the skull and top of the spine of the ancient thing was wrapped all about by a green, squid-like creature.

"A Nerve-Cyst, controlling the corpse after death." She whispered, and stamped down hard on it. She caught a glimpse of herself in her gun sight reflection, and wiped away a lipstick smear, delighted with how good she looked despite the desperate circumstance.

That means every stiff all the way down could have a spine-goobly, waiting to make it jump out at me in the dark. Trying not to despair, she said a prayer to Holy Fjordstrom and thought back to the events which had left her in this situation...

She was a successful treasure-hunter, scouring the galaxy with her boyfriend, Jimmy, for rare and exotic finds. They had heard about Redbeard's disastrous 'Lich' misadventure during his exploration of the catacombs of the Greater Crab asteroid. Their hunt had mentioned 'vast rare mineral reserves' and their ears picked up immediately.

Their ship was fast, but when they got there another treasure hunter had already arrived ahead of them — Elfina had stamped her foot to see it was Jimmy's jealous ex-girlfriend: Jazmin.

Jazmin had blocked the main southern entrance to the old mine with her large, sleek corsair. She was a crazy, rich bitch and a real weapon. They had feigned friendliness, baiting Jazmin (with her gratingly open fondness for Jimmy) to let them aboard, to talk collaboration, as Jimmy had the only known map of the old mine. She acquiesced and they all spent some cordial time onboard the corsair, making plans. But soon after Elfina had caught them making love on the sly in the storage bay.

"Cheater!" She had cried, "She's a whore Jimmy!" But Jazmin had just attacked her, throwing a punch, and Elfina had Judo-flipped her into a glass bar, smashing it to pieces along with several expensive bottles of spirits. They had scuffled in this mess for a while, smashing bottles over one another.

When Elfina had tried to flee back to their ship, Jimmy had grabbed her arms, and when she pushed him away he accidentally fell into Jazmin's acidic mineral-artifact bath.

Jazmin had become even crazier at this and tried to shoot Elfina with a Megatuna-harpoon, which hit the atomic-reverser and started a fire on the corsair. Elfina eventually bettered the hussy by applying a thigh-lock at the neck, until Jazmin passed out. Then Elfina quickly checked her hair and got into the airlock in time, as the horrific skinless ghoul that had been Jimmy emerged from the baths, mumbling "Elfina! I love you Elfina!" from a melted death's-face. The ship's atomic engine began to break apart, sending energy bolts arcing about the interior.

It was good while it lasted, Jimmy. She had thought, and escaped luckily on the ship's aft, facing the catacomb entrance. Redbeard's team had set up a satellite which provided a false atmosphere and oxygen on the asteroid, which was fortunate as her space suit was already in tatters and her skin sticky with booze. She was going in — she would be damned if she was going to waste a treasure-hunting trip just because her boyfriend was dead and the way back to their ship blocked.

She had blasted the seal over the entrance — crudely erected by local authorities after the Redbeard disaster. But as she entered the old mine she had to shoot some giant waterbears and asteroid-centipedes and other creepy crawlies.

"Shoo!" She had cried, exterminating every last one, leaving the entrance a charred and smoking maw, before walking into the darkness...

"Now here I am." She whispered pouting as she watched the last licks of flame die-down on the rags of the blasted mummy. "I'll find Redbeard's treasure. That cheater Jimmy would have wanted me to find it, had he lived. He said he loved me."

She rounded another corner and saw nothing, just that the stairs ahead split left and right. She tried to recall in her mind the map Jimmy had shown her, and after considering, went left. Her flashlight began to reflect a shine upon the ground — a large slime trail. *Ew.* She turned around and went right.

Eventually Elfina came to a strange section where the stair walls seemed coated in a kind of crystal, almost like ice, but it was not cold. She noticed then that not all the mummy alcoves were filled here, and those that were had unmummified and recently deceased habitants. The wall to one side was open to another yawning chasm, with the sound of distant wind howling.

Definitely members of Redbeard's team. She mused, studying the newer additions through the crystal seal. She passed by one with only a very thin veneer of crystal, it was like looking at someone frozen in a river. The man was young and handsome with a short but virile copper-blonde beard. To her surprise, as she shone her flashlight in, his green eyes darted towards her, the pupils shrinking. Elfina gave a quick shriek, then setting her blaster to the lowest setting, she stepped back and began to melt him out. But she had only begun the process, and heard the crystal cracking, when there was a groan in her ear, and the wrapped, skeletal arms of one of the wall-mummies embraced her in a bear hug. She grunted with strain, hoping her own ribs weren't cracking, as the thing was surprisingly strong for a bag of bones. Her shooting arm was locked down, and the mummies clacking teeth were trying to get past her voluminous hair at her smooth and exposed neck. She noticed another mummy shuffling towards her as well, and she began to feel a resignation that this would be the end.

Suddenly a fist shot out of the wall, the handsome young man had been freed by her melting shot just enough to release one arm, and with this he grabbed the thing's forelimb and pulled hard, breaking the bones in a shower of dust. Elfina took her chance, sliding her gun arm free and shooting the thing's head off. The cyst parasite within was burst open and burned, and gruesome black goo from it splattered the ground. With a "Hiyah!" she jump-kicked the headless body into the open chasm, to drop for untold lengths of time.

The other mummy took the curious approach of groping her, its skeletal hands grabbing at the frilly lace of her bra. "Creep!" She exclaimed as it squeezed her ample bosom, and a flash of the plasma pistol lit up her grimacing face, as she blew out the groper's rib cage, igniting his insides and immolating him in a fierce blaze.

She heard a strange sound, like the primordial bark of some kind of enormous animal, echoing up from the open drop, and her beautiful eyes went very wide, and met the trapped man's green eyes, and she quickly finished melting his confines. He was tall, svelte and shirtless with shiny silver excavation trousers and boots still intact. She felt vulnerable, brushing the mummy-dust off her limbs, which now glistened with sweat, then helped him brush the crystal-powder off his. As the tall man came free he quickly stamped on the Nerve-Cyst which had escaped the burning mummy, as it was probing the stone floor for a new host.

"My name is Ohm." He said in a surprisingly calm and mildly accented deep voice.

"I'm Elfina." She said, seeing he too was strained and exhausted, and wanting the comfort of human contact she embraced him, and quickly became aware of their mutual near-nakedness. As they pressed together they felt more alive than ever in the varieties of pressing dangers, and ignoring all intelligent instinct to move on quickly, they began kissing one another passionately, until he made love to her on the cavern stair.

Suddenly a sound distracted them, and wheeling with her torch Elfina caught once more the rapid flutter of movement darting away around the next bend. She caught a better look this time, and thought she saw similar silver boots and trousers to those Ohm wore.

"They are the creatures of the Lich now," Ohm said. "They are the ones who imprisoned me, though they hadn't yet infected me. Everything here, living and dead, is infected with a Nerve-Cyst and obeys the Lich. The Lich is the Queen-Cyst." Ohm took her hand, "We must find a way out." She was entranced by Ohm's strength and charisma.

From behind them, there came a loud shriek: "You bitch!" They heard, followed by a loud plasma blast. It struck Ohm in the torso, and his arms and legs went flying as he was incinerated.

Eflina saw Jazmin there, still in a space-suit, and aiming a large blaster-rifle. "The treasure will be mine, you cow," Jazmin said and shot again, blowing apart a section of wall. Elfina found herself running ahead at full speed, rounding the bend and charging downward for several minutes, leaping two and three steps at a time, her emotions a wild confusion of having just met a man, loved him, and lost him. She stumbled hard and rolled for an incredible distance, until the stair rounded a corner over one of the open chasms, and she tumbled over the edge into the darkness.

She did not fall too far, however, landing in a strange nest of old tools and metal engineering pieces. A crudely-made mining robot came to life in the nest, making electronic squawks, its mouth and eyes glowing red in its brown-rusted head. She couldn't imagine the purpose of the thing, but it looked old and weird. It seemed to find her presence exciting and began desperate attempts to speak in a broken electronic voice:

"Ah, yes at last, I am still available for all mineral testing needs, yes there's no problem there, no issues with me whatsover. I mean I seem to have lost my legs and my equipment but that's nothing to an old star-dog toolbox like me. I must say you are rather striking, quite a sight to old rusted eyes like mine, how did you arrive here? Plopping out of the sky like a falling cherry? Can I ask your name? I mean we'll need to stick together..."

She found the thing instantly irritating and creepy, and looked over the side. She discovered she was on a small ledge overlooking the great black chasm. The stairs she had been following wound gradually downward in a spiral about this chasm, so that she saw she could rejoin it in a leap across the void. A bit far, and a bit of a drop, but almost do-able in a good jump.

The bot continued its chatter: "I know I'm not much to look at but with my brains and your... beauty, I mean we could make a little paradise in this ah, wretched... filthy... nest-thing..."

She considered shooting it, when she heard Jazmin somewhere above her: "Where are you bitch?" And saw a light rounding the corner she had rolled off. Elfina raised a warning finger, and the bot fell silent. Then Jazmin was gone, following the winding stair, and Elfina looked back across the drop. *If I can make that jump I'll be ahead of Jazmin by a good bit.*

She heard the distant primordial barking again, somewhere down in the dark, and thought *I'm done for anyway,* and she prepared to fling herself across the void.

Then she saw him. He walked out of the shadows on the stairs she was aiming for, across the divide. The thing she had caught a glimpse of twice already, dressed as one of Redbeard's team, what Ohm had called the creature of the Lich. It was like a little partially decomposed man with a curly red beard, and she knew instantly it was Redbeard himself, and that this was not his real name, but a nickname. He spoke then:

"You won't make it you know. The Lich is all-powerful here. Why even try? Just join us, it's not so bad. We could use you." Redbeard's mouth was black, as were his eyes.

"Hey I met her first pal..." the bot started yammering.

"You have intelligence?" She said to Redbeard. "Do you remember your name?"

The walking corpse only smiled, grimly, and she continued, "why would I choose to live down in this gross pit?" She began to check her hair and lipstick again in the reflection of her gun's telescopic sight.

"You won't wish to live elsewhere. The Lich provides all, down here he is a god. When you are put to rest and the cyst-worm shows you the truth, you will agree."

"Your look like a little rotting leprechaun..." While still pretending to check her hair she had casually aimed her gun directly at him without his noticing. She quickly shot little Elmer Redbeard in half. His animated corpse was devoid of blood, just dry guts, His upper half, still controlled by the nerve-cyst, slithered off into the dark making little mewling sounds.

"Oh bravo," the bot chattered, "I'm so glad you did that, what a shot! LIsten, I hope I'm not coming on too strong but..." Not wasting any time, she made the jump across the chasm.

She landed hard on the stair of the far side, boots-first, but rolled and tumbled out of control. *Might have sprained my ankle slightly, but nothing broken.* She had rolled too far to the other side and slipped over that edge, her voluptuous white hips vanishing down an open shaft of some kind which narrowed to a rounded tunnel, guiding her downward rapidly like a long *stone slide*. She slid down this a long way before being spat out a mouth-like chute into a vast open cavern. She fell through the open air to land with a soft bounce on a large marshmallowy asteroid fungus, causing her to flop several more times up in the air before coming to rest.

The giant cavern was well-lit, from some industrial source, with a small fireball acting as a pretend sun. The air was busy with noise and activity. Almost comically she could see then the Perambulator Lich. It was a gargantuan Nerve-Cyst, bigger than several men, sitting upon a stone throne like a lardy leech. It seemed to wear a giant Moltard skull as a kind of mask or crown, emulating a humanoid. It sat near to the fake sun, attended to by mummies. Beneath its throne was a vast dry lake of bones and rusted metal instruments.

"Eeewwww.." She said, immediately reaching for her blaster. But the fungus she was sitting on has begun to absorb her. *A sex-shroom!* She realized. They were notoriously amorous and semi-sentient space fungi, who could psychically influence their prey in a faux courtship — resulting in the prey's digestion.

Pretty, pretty, pretty, she could hear the horrid thing's thoughts in her brain as its hard jelly-like surface began to suck at her, drawing her into it. But her absorbed gun-hand still had the finger on the trigger, and she squeezed off a shot. *Pain, pain, pain!* Was the new thought it projected and it spat her off with a flapping sphincter sound. She landed on her feet, looking quickly about her. The thing had absorbed the sound of the shot, she had not yet been detected.

She noticed immediately a scintillating array of rough-cut minerals and jewels among the sex-shrooms, which were also everywhere at all sizes from tiny to enormous. She could see where the stairs she had been following ended, and about these awaited a small army of Lich-zombies. There were mummies, miners, former members of Redbeard's team, and weird animals and mutants of all description. There was even some recent adventurers that had beaten her here, freshly turned to minions of the horrid buttery maggot sitting upon the throne. Some of the men were still armed with blasters.

That stair is impassable. Nobody has made it this far before me. She realized the mishap of her fall had changed everything, and saved her life. She noticed something else as well. *Quadrapene crystals,* unmistakable in their dark-blood colour, lined the floor and walls of the cavern. *One of the universe's most rare and valuable resources. A piece the size of my head could buy me a planet, and it's everywhere.*

Being a clever girl, and realizing her incredible luck, she wasted no time, and after checking what remained of her make-up, she clicked a button on her blaster which extended the long range barrel, and resting her arm on a giant Moltard femur, aimed carefully across the cavern. A thin beam sliced through the air and into the unsuspecting Lich's lardy middle. It immediately emitted a high pitched shriek, and vibrated horribly, as its yellow and black innards spilled out of her snipers incision. She clicked another button, activating the explosive shot, and sending this directly into the gaping wound, the blubbery thing exploded in a fiery rain of fat and slime.

With that, all the infected creatures throughout the mine became listless and leaderless and began to disband — all seeking to nest themselves in wall-alcoves and rest in oblivious hibernation, having lost with their king their sentience.

Elfina found an old miners backpack, and taking up as much Quadrapene crystal as she could carry, made her way back up the stair.

On the way back she came across Jazmin, who was still in her space suit, but the glass of her helmet was smashed. Jazmin's eyes were white, and Elfina could see the pinkish leech-tail of a cyst still at her neck, which was burrowing into her brain as Jazmin robotically placed herself into a mummy's alcove in the wall between two others.

"Serves you right, slut." Elfina said, briefly checking her hair in the cracked glass of Jazmin's helmet, before making her way back out of the mine.She emerged from the expedition with the greatest treasure horde since the LeBlanc GoldBrain find. She became so wealthy that she could buy her own small moon and rule there as royalty. She discovered soon after that the handsome mystery-man Ohm had impregnated her, and she gave birth to a strong son, named Ohm, who one day became moon-king.

Well, Elfina sounds like a very sexy lady. Ramek would also have impregnated her, only he probably would not have died. Ramek is not so easy to kill. Ramek would also like to be a moon-king. Where in the galaxy can I find this woman? Ramek will marry her, dethrone her son, and reimpregnate her with a king so powerful he will rule the galaxy.

The Map of Heaven
Jason Lupus

The Strange Legacy of Professor Blake Anderson, as accounted by his close colleague and friend, Alexander Milton.

Professor Barry Anderson was a genius of many scientific fields as well as a close personal friend of mine. His varied interests included mysticism, mathematics, astronomy, architecture, engineering, painting, and psychedelic expeditions of the personal consciousness.

Anderson lived on the very outskirts of civil society, at the edges of the Arizona desert. He lived in a geodesic dome house of his own design (with Persian geometrical stained glass) which was also his laboratory. Quite alone. I'm not sure why he never took a wife, he had a variety of partners available from his cult following, but he opted for solitude. Sad, in a way, but that's how he preferred it. I expect he wanted nothing at all to interfere with his studies and explorations.

Periodically, his unusual colleagues would undertake visits from Phoenix. I had been there several times when they would arrive — a massive dust-storm desert convoy of motorcycles and muscle cars. They would arrive at his laboratory already half-spaced on various psychotropes, emerging like a strange army from dirt-road clouds through the fierce heat. You can imagine the colourfulness of these occasions. Though many of these were biker psychonauts, many were students of physics, psychology, philosophy, and magick, and came to Anderson for scientific inquiry and spiritual advice. He was to them a guru or shaman.

His dome-laboratory was quite isolated and surrounded by a calming vista of mountains, cactuses and sand. His pride and joy, despite the various recreational facilities (like his natural rock-pool and home gymnasium) was his sensory deprivation tank. This he had made from an old bomb shelter, in the shadow of the dome. The door to it was painted with an ouroboros (with a fire inside the serpent-circle).

Anderson once spoke to me about how yogic retreats in the desert he had visited as a student had inspired the nature of his outpost-laboratory. It was during such a retreat that Garuda, the mythical bird-deity of oriental lore, visited him in the night and told him to build a center for 'inner-space exploration'. That once he had done so, he would be able to create of his mind a 'harpoon'. I can only say this is how Anderson described it to me. But yes, a harpoon, as he put it, by which he meant a form for his mind in the astral plane, and this astral harpoon could then be launched through the multitude of heavens and hells. According to this vision, this would enable him to get a cohesive record of the vastness of esoteric cosmology. To plan a route through the astral labyrinth of heavens and hells, and return to reality with a kind of map for inner-space exploration.

Anderson truly believed in this vision from the start. He never detailed to me the exact events of his early yogic retreats, but I know he fervently believed this dream and seeing it to its conclusion was a staple of all his life's work since that time.

During the dreadfully hot summer of 2028 Anderson asked a couple of his colleagues, including myself, to accompany him for what he sold to us as witnessing his 'penultimate inner-space exploration' in his sensory deprivation tank. I knew his experiments were not always safe, and if he was inviting his scientific colleagues like me and not the usual gang of bikers, then it was something serious.

From what I can recall in his e-mail requesting my presence, Anderson expressed at that time something akin to this sentiment, though I have forgotten the exact words and lost the e-mail: "Soon, religion and science shall expand further, but in unison. Replacing the fractured religious and scientific understanding of today. Hopefully broadening the awareness of humanity, revealing what lies beyond the Olympian gates."

When the date came, I arrived at his home with my wife. There was only a small handful of people there, among them I was surprised to recognize a biker from one of the larger parties, by the unique name of 'Go-Zone'. He was grizzled and dirty, like he'd been wandering in the desert alone, and wearing jeans and leather despite the heat. He smiled at me from behind tinted glasses and a dirty doo-rag. I recalled him then as a thoughtful fellow, extremely interested in Anderson's studies. He must have made some kind of impression upon the Professor, and was now a trusted confidant. Go-Zone was giving offerings and prayers to Anderson's Garuda shrine. He told me Anderson had allowed him into the tank, and had shown him the first level of hell, and a tiny glimpse of heaven beyond. I'll never forget that conversation. There was one other person invited, an anthropologist by the name of Giza, but this person was too painfully and autistically shy to even introduce himself to us.

We were greeted warmly and well hosted by Anderson, enjoying a dinner which in some ways felt like a 'last meal', despite the air of friendly company there was also a deadly seriousness about the occasion. I honestly at that time expected nothing more than the usual monitoring of the tank for a night, followed by a recording of Anderson's experience. While I was deeply interested, I was frankly always agnostic about his revelations.

That night Anderson decided to enter his sensory deprivation tank. He was naked save for some strange Celtic and oriental-looking patterns he had painted on himself in blue, and my wife blushed at this. I dare say she wondered what kind of madness I had gotten her into, but she was at least amused by Anderson and Go-Zone, and by the calm of the place itself.

The good Professor said to us then: "The paradigms, I should say the path, that I return with shall shatter our grounded concept of reality, for the greater good of humanity. These metaphysical discoveries you, my closest allies, are about to be a part of, shall in a single leap and bound evolve the consciousness of the human race towards a self-aware near-godhood. For there can only be a revolutionizing of metaphysics and material reality when one possesses a material map to navigate the hidden worlds beyond the veil of sleep. Beyond the valley of death."

I recall clearly, despite being quite affected myself by the peyote we had already mutually ingested, that his sensory deprivation tank had pink and purple lights, going off and on. I cannot say their purpose, perhaps just to be trippy. I recall also the beauty of the desert night sky, the stars shining down upon us, and in through his dome-house. After he entered Go-Zone yelled "Right on, man," and left him to do some drinking. Go-Zone was unsurprisingly just the type of person one wants around on such occasions.

After some time, I went back to the deprivation chamberto check on him. Things had changed.

There were brilliant flashes occurring, nothing like the electric pink and purple artificial lights, but *emanating from the tank itself!* They were like bolts of lightning blasting away in there, and the odd one came shooting out from the tank. I saw it strike a cactus in the distance, which then began burning in a greenish flame. More oddly there was a strange kind of howling, which at first I thought was the wind behaving strangely, but after the other events which occurred I'm not quite sure. I think the cactus itself was howling lonesomely.

I remember saying to Go-Zone: "Can you see this?"
"Yeah man," was all he replied.

As these flashes continued they would light up the entire bunker like an X-ray, and Go-Zone pointed out with a yell that we could see, briefly, the terrain Anderson was travelling for a brief instant during these. I did indeed see a spear or harpoon moving over a bizarre landscape, like a mountainous terrain but made of space and stars and nebula, folded and forming fiery hills and dales. I saw giant floating embryos and foetuses' in burning sacs, drifting in the aether of this domain. I will attest that Go-Zone and even my wife, who had taken no peyote, all saw the same thing in those flashes.

Astral mountains, and skies of fire and water. We saw other things, as we watched in rapt disbelief: realms of the dead, in untold multitudes and numbers, crossing giant rafts and barks, and dark pyramids within which I sensed there lived gods. Or at least a force which we must call God. Their power, in just a second's illuminating flash, was so formidable that my hands shake at the memory to this day, at the untouchable sense of power.

My wife fainted at one of these, and concerned for her safety I rushed her into the dome, and saw no more visions.

There was at last a flash so brilliantly bright that it lit everything up even within the dome.I laid my wife on the couch, realizing she had only fainted, and rushing back outside I saw the ground around the bomb shelter hazed with dust and smoke. There was no sign of Go-Zone, who I never saw or heard from again, and found no records as to his family name or real identity. All that remained of him that I could find was a blackened biker boot.

Eventually professor Anderson began banging on the tank, and I nervously opened the hatch and helped him out carefully. His body seemed strangely contorted, his eyes incredibly wild, and he made sounds as though he was desperate to talk with me, but could no longer form the words. When I brought him inside my wife was awake, and she screamed at the sight of the professor, as he went into a state of unconsciousness in my arms, and we were forced to rush him to the hospital.

Once there, and under care, what happened to him is a matter of record. All apart from the testimony I am writing here. From his hospital bed he would periodically awaken, briefly, before slipping back into a coma. While awake he would draw and write details of the hells and heavens his astral body had traveled through, beyond the gates of Olympus. Soaring above the realm of those watchful, immortal deities. He could no longer speak, only draw.

Anderson had trouble even writing words, but he managed to get to me some scrawled notes, during one of my visits, and I could see it took all of his energy to commit. The top note said simply: "Map — in the drawings. The legions of souls, circle the wheel forever. A great one, an immortal, spoke to me. Told me my mission on earth was now accomplished, but that nothing will change." He handed me with this some drawings, in the hopes I would expand upon them, I think, but they seemed indecipherable.

Once I left the hospital that night I was told the Professor had passed away. The notes he had passed to me were soon considered of sacred esoteric value to his many followers, and his hero-worship as a scientific mystic only grew. I myself became a person of great interest to those people, and I must say I have had many interactions with numbers of them since, both desperate and unwelcome as well as enlightening and friendly.

Of these notes I have yet been unable to piece together a 'map'. Despite getting the help of other leading astral psychonauts. There is but one page of his notes that is clear and suggestive, and that has a crude drawing of an eyeball, and a series of mountain ranges and rivers, over which is scribbled a route, as typical as any other map. At the edge of this he drew an end to the land, and waves describing an ocean, and in that ocean what seem like dead people floating or swimming. He left an arrow here pointing upwards, with scrawled letters that appear to maybe say: 'the eagle'.

After this my friend Anderson became a kind of folk-legend in the Arizona region. His dome-laboratory, with his nearby grave, have become a site of sacred pilgrimage. And the caravans of esoteric adventurers still arrive there en masse in billowing dust bowls and the sound of roaring engines. I have yet to go back, and doubt I will, for my dreams remain plagued by his words about 'the immortal one' and that feeling I had when I saw the pyramid in the star-scape.

The bikers constructed a shrine to Dr. Blake Anderson, in order to commemorate his legacy. And here they still leave offerings, which are picked up and blown across the plain by the desert winds.

Ramek recommends that you do not use drugs, kiddies. There will be plenty of time for psychic exploration when death opens its door to you.

Max Ryan: Hunter and Hunted

By Luke O'Donnell

Max Ryan: Hunter and Hunted

Max Ryan and his team had been dumped into the spore-forest.

The wilds of Horka's World were dense with above-ground mushroom growth — where they rose and morphed into twisted tree-like shapes, resembling dry-land sea anemones. About these grew vegetation, evolved from algae, resembling vines which surrounded the fungus and knotted together the forest into a dense bracket which was hell to traverse.

Beneath the purplish skies of Horka's World Ryan's group had cut a trail through a river valley, making their way to an old temple complex: a cyclopean pyramidal structure which overlooked the valley. It was almost totally overgrown with spore-trees and vines, and Ryan looked up at this now as the purplish twilight fell. His keen green eyes took in every detail as he moved his cigar from one corner of his mouth to the other.

The dense growth left Ryan feeling claustrophobic — endless walls of thick, wood-like fungus, white or tan or chalky blue, covered in a quick-growing humid vegetation which wrapped everything, including the ground, with leaves that retreated at night. The branches became somewhat hard, like a pulpy wood, difficult to cut through. The air was full of travelling clouds of spore-dust, and strange birds resembling giant bugs.

The density had reduced Ryan's visible range to just a few metres. The heat of the place disrupted the thermal vision in his ocular implants as well as sapped his energy. Likewise the sensors on his suit were rendered useless, unable to differentiate between the creaking spore-trees or scurrying small animals and any genuine hostile threat that might be lurking around the next arbor. He scratched the long scar that ran down his face.

His well-honed instinct was his last detection system. *Luckily it was his best.*

Of course he was never without augmentation. He had developed denser muscle and bone through steroids and surgery, his eyes were tech replacements. As far as humans go, he was a killing machine. As he worked his way through the dense forest he thought back to his training days, many years previous:

"There is no better sensor than the MK1 eyeball." He had been designed, educated, and trained from day one to trust no one — not himself, not his superiors, not their plans. Everything was counter-tested, to its limit, and half the time he was unsure which side he was fighting for, in the various power struggles of the system and wars both cold and hot.

While Ryan and his security patrol ran overlapping sweeps of the dense undergrowth, the company science team they were escorting followed just behind them. The mission to this hell-planet had been surprisingly smooth so far, and Ryan felt tempted to surmise his employment with Speculatore would be an easy ride.

Ha! He gave a snorting smirk at his own girlish optimism before chomping down harder on his cigar. Of course it would be hard and bitter, like all the other jobs. Probably even more so, considering how things had been so far. He rubbed his scarred and square-jawed chin and ran his hand over his buzz-cut scalp.

His recruitment with the organisation had consisted of them tranquillising, black-bagging, and smuggling him off earth to Speculatore's headquarters in mega-caves beneath Mars. "Not the friendliest introduction," he thought. But he'd had worse.

They revealed things to him then which made him sympathetic to their aims. The galaxy was a war of corporations and none were much morally different from another. They had shown him an alien artifact, deep in the bowels of Mars, which had further softened his attitude towards them, as they specialised in such compelling research. So now he was a company man.

Ryan continued onwards, still chewing his cigar, refocusing his mind on the patrol at hand. A large centipede-like creature dropped from a wide vine-leaf onto his forearm. Ryan studied it for a moment, how its many legs glowed different colours, before blowing smoke on it and squashing it against a thick trunk of vine.

Blue blood.

"You grunts are destroying a pristine jungle of undocumented flora and fauna." It was Sanchez, the organisation's chief Xeno-Historian. He had been breaking Ryan's balls since the start. *Little-guy envy.*

"Could be poisonous." Ryan said.

"Here's a bigger one." Ryan's number one, Fletcher, said, using his rifle to draw one twice the size off the back of Sanchez, who immediately went pale. They both stared at him waiting to see if he would step on the thing, but to his credit he kept walking, his eyes darting to the canopy of weirdness above them.

"Why do they call this place Horka's World?" Fletcher asked Sanchez.

"Named for the guy who discovered it." Ryan interjected.

"The first guy to land here?"

"No, the first to see it in a space-telescope, boy. Any luck finding a clearing yet, where we might get a retrieval drop ship?"

"Nothing yet sir."

The team had been tasked with investigating the ancient temple located in the unexplored wilds at the planet's equatorial belt, at the heart of its single supercontinent. So far the mission had gone off without a hitch, there had been a few run-ins with some local predators, a very large bug-bird and a few creatures that resembled dog-sized rockfish with legs that lept out of burrowed ambush holes in the vine-covered ground. But these foes they'd manage to ward off with gunfire and flares. Ryan noticed a pattern of the fish-dogs to nest near certain spore-trees, and they learned to avoid them entirely. Ryan had good instinct s for dealing with animals, especially predators.

Their journey along the ravine, following the strange violet-coloured stream, now brought them to the base of the hill which housed the ancient temple — their target. Ryan kept scanning the area for a clearing suitable for the drop ship.

"It will have to be at the temple itself, from the roof." He finally said to Fletcher, and they began a long march up the hill. The overgrowth was thicker than ever. As they marched, Ryan overheard the conversation between Sanchez and his company of scientists.

"....Clear signs of previous habitation!" Exclaimed Sanchez, stopping to pick up fragments of something from the ground, dusting off thousands of years of dust.

"It's near irrelevant at this point, we found nothing of value to us." Replied his assistant, Steiner.

"That's all we care about? What's useful to us?" Anger overtook Sanchez as he raised his voice at Steiner and the others. "The questions of this temple's origins have enormous scientific and historic importance! Signs of an advanced civilization, possibly star-fairing, existing on this planet over five hundred thousand years ago. Leaving no trace of itself other than this site! And what's more, a civilization that may have vanished due to regression to barbarism."

Ryan looked over to Fletcher at this, a thoughtful look on his face. He rolled his cigar on his teeth.

Suddenly there was an order from his wrist security screen to get down. Ryan had felt something was not right about a second before, and had put his hand on Fletcher's shoulder. Something had tripped the scanners in close proximity to them, the whole team was alerted.

Ryan scanned his surroundings, using every piece of instinct he had. The read on the scanners had been large, bigger than a man, but incredibly brief. It was a mere flash — but now the equipment was not reading anything. Ryan himself could see and hear nothing, nor could the other security operatives, but deep in his core Ryan felt the unease of being stalked. The hair on his tanned and well-worn skin was standing on end as he partially climbed a fungus tree, trying to see any kind of further view. But he saw nothing, and nothing happened.

The men continued to scan the ghostly forest in all directions, hearts hammering in their chests.

Still nothing.

Too quiet for the planet's predators, but also no sign of an ambush by a sentient foe. These thoughts raced through Ryan's mind.

"Could it be one of them?" Sanchez asked.

"Who?" Fletcher replied.

"Evecorp, Orion, Ward Limited?"

"The rival corporations? Hiring hit men, leaving booby traps?" Fletcher asked.

"Anything but an animal would have riddled us with fire by now," Ryan said, ending this speculation.
Drowning out the background noise of the alien forest animals around him, Ryan tried to focus on anything out of the ordinary, his instincts still screaming at him.

Nothing.

After what seemed like an eternity he gave the stand-down order.

"Must have been a falling branch or something" he announced over his radio. "But stay alert." His instincts were still telling them that they were in danger. He knew well to trust them, but without evidence he could not keep them from advancing. And either way, they were safer on higher ground. From the top of that structure they might be able to see for miles. *One of us might need to get taken out in order to reveal this threat*, he also thought, and pushed his feelings down as he continued his patrol.

The group continued uphill, progressing slowly. Now no one was talking, as a deep sense of paranoia had set in, and every creaking branch and animal call caused a sense of alarm. Ryan was the only one capable of keeping a calm demeanor, but he knew better than anyone that they were about to get hit.

"Something's really wrong here." He whispered to Sanchez and Steiner as they marched, wanting to warn the non-military team. The thought just wouldn't get out of his mind, no matter how many times he checked and rechecked his surroundings. "I have no proof, just be ready."

Sanchez, almost unbelievably, remained preoccupied with some of the archaeological finds he had made. He seemed to be focusing on one fragment, trying to translate or decipher some raised symbols.

The valley contained numerous smaller streams which ran down the hills to join like arteries into the flow of the main river that had bored through the rock to create the valley. It was while they were crossing one of these streams that the first attack finally came.

Ryan heard a scream of terror from the rear-most position. He turned in time to see one of his security guards hauled upwards and backwards into one of the mushroom trees by an unseen force.

It's Renton! Ryan had a moment to realize, before ducking as Renton squeezed the trigger of his rifle in blind panic, sending a hail of gunfire down on the rest of the group. The hypersonic rounds sent everyone diving for cover, blowing the arm off of one of Sanchez's egghead aides.

One bullet exploded a hair's breadth from Ryan's head as it detonated against a tree, showering his short-cropped hair in spore-dust as he squinted and spat out his cigar. It was over in seconds. Someone had tried to fire on the attacker, but Renton was gone, without anyone even seeing what it was.

Ryan had a feeling, like it had been the same colour as the chalky trees.

He moved to rally his unit, tightening his lines of fire and keeping the scientists in the centre of a circle of armed men. The shredded corpse of Renton suddenly fell from the canopy and landed near to them with a splatter of gore, the bright red a stark and alien colour among the muted pastel tones of the alien world.

“Call your targets!” Ryan screamed as his men closed ranks. He lit another cigar, slowly looking back and forth. Their unseen foe had disappeared again, leaving only a corpse.

Moving to inspect the body, Ryan squinted as he examined it, hearing Sanchez gag and vomit. Renton had been torn apart with such force that his armour and exoskeleton struts had been ripped along with his bone. *Something powerful.*

“This looks like animal claw marks, but the cuts are too clean, whatever did this had claws sharper than monoblades and the strength to match.” Ryan explained to the group.

“It didn’t eat him, so it’s out to kill, not hunt us for food. We are trophies, gentlemen.”

Sanchez pushed forward, recovering himself, but looking quite panicked: “There’s no animal on this planet that could do this, and why didn’t we detect it? Anything bigger than a fly would be picked up on the thermals!”

“Some creatures can regulate their own body temperatures.” Ryan offered.

Steiner joined in agreement. “Yes, maybe this is something similar? An undiscovered species perhaps?”

“Doesn’t matter.” Snapped Ryan, “we need to get this moving feast to the extraction point now!”

“The temple...” Sanchez said, and looked again to his artifact. Ryan wondered if he was losing it.

With this the team continued along up the hillside, praying that there would be a walkable clearing just beyond the next thicket. But their unseen stalker followed them, hurling large rocks and logs at the team, testing their defensive perimeter constantly and attempting to wear the team’s nerves down. One of the scientists was crushed by a log, his neck broken.

Hushed conversation continued amongst the team as they darted from position to position, cutting and hacking as they went. The progress was unbelievably slow and their nerves were shattered. "We are approaching the breaking point" Ryan thought.

But instinct overtook him as his foe made another lightning strike. A near supersonic blur of movement barrelled past Ryan, sending him flying. This was followed by a sickening crunch of teeth on flesh and the sound of bones being broken to splinters. Another of the party, Steiner, had been eviscerated in a cloud of pink mist as the group split apart in panic.

Scrambling to his feet, Ryan moved with lightning speed, sending a burst of fire into the mushroom jungle as the stalker retreated. Cycling through his vision settings Ryan caught the briefest outline of a blur in motion, about 8 feet tall in height, long tailed, chalky and pale like most things of the planet. It seemed to have a ridge of hair all along its spine, and in the brief second his augmented eyes noted that portions of the things flesh changed colour, adapting camouflage based on what it was passing. Gathering the remains of the team he noticed that in addition to the unlucky Steiner, another of the security detachment was missing, presumably dragged off to his doom by the creature.

"But now I know how I can see it," he whispered to Fletcher, and began to hatch a plan.

Moving quickly, the security detail tightened the perimeter around the science team and under Ryan's orders they switched to electromagnetic scanning frequencies, while continuing the march to the temple, all the time facing outwards and remaining alert.

Ryan pushed them hard. "Get to the top, NOW!" He kept yelling, smiting their backs and hacking away the strange trees the most ardently. Eventually they reached the base of the temple, long buried in layers of the chalky soil, wrapped all about with vines, with mushroom trees growing all across its length, sides, and summit. Yet the structure was of such gargantuan scope that it was still visible, and impressive. They found a route up its wall, and eventually even some vine-covered stairs. Sanchez desperately took visual recordings of the wall symbols as they advanced, though Ryan repeatedly shoved him forward with his rifle butt.

"Time enough for your studies if we survive, big-brain."

Exhausted and torn to shreds by branches, they finally reached the temple summit. This too was lined with tall fungus-trees, but there were clear areas for a lander to make ground, and Ryan made the call. There was no answer, and he looked up to Sanchez, who was eyeing him with a desperate cynicism.

But then there was a series of awful screams, and running to their source, they found the ground and trunks of white fungus-trees stained red with blood.

"Who was here, how many?" Ryan yelled, and Fletcher was there, his arm bleeding badly. "It was here, it cut me sir, it was so fast. It took three of our guys, in the blink of an eye, I didn't even get a shot!"

"Ryan...." Sanchez said quietly, staring at his artifact.

"Wait, be quiet..." Ryan was looking upwards, studying with his augmented eyes.

"Ryan!"

"Be quiet, or I will kill you."

"Ryan it's them. It's one of them."

"One of what?"

"One of the race who built the temple, what's left of them. They reverted to this, to this animal state. They were once more intelligent than us, Ryan."

"So what are you saying? He's too precious to kill?"

Sanchez just lowered his head, shaking it back and forth.

"Okay then, now be silent." Ryan raised his arm, and everyone became quiet and looked about them. He was still looking up, to the trees above them. Amongst the foliage, perched like a vulture up a thick mushroom-tree branch, Ryan finally caught a clear look at the beast. It sat there, motionless, staring him dead in his eyes, just covered enough to deny him a clear shot. In his electromagnetic sights, Ryan noticed the faint shimmer around it. "A strange magnetic shield of some kind. Might protect from bullets." Ryan knew what he had to do.

Relaying this information to his remaining squad, he prepared a smart smoke grenade in his shoulder launcher, setting it to disrupt the field.

"Stay frosty, it's going to strike again soon."

The stalker made its move: hurling another branch to the group's left as a feint, it dropped from its perch and charged from the right.

"Getting predictable" Ryan thought as he fired his shoulder mount directly into his predicted path for the beast. "Just another wild animal."

The smart smoke grenade burst a foot from the creature's face, unleashing a cloud of nanites that sparked bright blue, sending flashes of lightning outward from the blast zone as they collapsed his strange bio-magnetic field. A pained scream pierced the jungle as the creature recoiled in agony.

Revealed in all its horror as it clawed at its own face, letting out hideous screeching the creature stumbled into full view of the group. It was pale, gangly, not enormously dissimilar from the fungus-trees it lived within. The thing's arms were too long for its size ending in claws longer than bayonets. There seemed to be algae growing on the thing's shoulders, and its hair-ridge was striped, like a zebras. It seemed reptilian in some ways, and in others almost humanoid, and Ryan caught the things eye for a moment. He was reminded at staring into the eye of an intelligent animal, like a porpoise or dog. That faint unmistakable moment of mutual sentient recognition — yet the thing was totally wild.

Momentarily distracted by shock, Ryan paused just long enough to give the stalker an opening. Before he came to his senses and opened fire, the beast pounced upon him from a distance impossible for any human or earth-animal to cross in such a time. The burst of fire from his rifle pattering off the beast's carapace as it lunged, but did not connect with anything vital. It barrelled into him, knocking him to the ground before trying to chew his neck out.

The panic in the group was instant with the security personnel unable to get a clear shot, as Ryan struggled with the beast like two roiling lions. Locking the joints on his exo-suit, Ryan jammed himself forward as his rifle was crushed by the creature's bulk. Reacting on pure instinct he jammed the useless weapon into the stalkers jaws before pushing it up and away from his face. The abomination clamped down hard on the weapon, crushing it between its vice like jaws and punching forward at him again.

In that tiny moment Ryan scrambled for his mono-blade while activating his compact combat buckler, the shield expanding just in time to take the blow from the creature's sword-like claws. Bringing the mono-blade upwards in a disembowelment strike, Ryan was parried with expert skill by the beast's claws, knocking aside his blade as it counter struck him.

It fights with almost human awareness and planning, he thought.

The pace of the fight was unbelievable, as the others watched in horror, with blows and counterblows being exchanged with expert skill. A shoulder slash here and stabbing thrust there, with each new strike and parry Ryan felt stamina drop, despite his enhanced biology and his exo-suit, the damage upon which was mounting with every passing moment. The beast seemed relentless and untiring, never flinching or weakening in the slightest. Ryan was getting desperate

I need to end this fast.

Ryan deliberately left his flank

open while slashing forward with his blade. The creature, reacting without hesitation, took the bait and drove one of its claws into his armour, scraping the knife-like talons into his ribs. It took all his discipline and self-control to ignore the searing explosion of agony in his side as he drove his leg in a downward kick, snapping the beast's ankle with a sickening crunch of bone. The beast seemed to speed up with fury and pain, but its attack lost balance, giving Ryan the edge he needed. With all his mechanically enhanced might he drove the short mono-blade sword into the beast's neck before kicking himself free and diving backwards to the ground. With this the air around him was filled with the distinct tearing fabric sound of the surviving team members' weapons opening up on full auto as they shot the thing to ribbons.

Thousands of rounds were expended in a few seconds as the creature was nearly turned inside out from the barrage of hypersonic explosive rounds, falling to the ground as a twitching carcass, leaking strange blue blood ichor onto the chalky ground.

Dusting himself off and walking back towards the team, Ryan lit another cigar. He realised then that the entire fight had lasted less than a minute from start to finish. The pain in his side flared as his wound was attended to by his Fletcher and another man. Fletcher's arm was also in a sling. Word came over the radio then, that air retrieval was on the way.

Sanchez's scientists looked at him in terror, he had just gone head to head with a monster of a forgotten age and lived to tell the tale. All except Sanchez himself, who had moved to inspect what remained of the thing's body. Joining him Ryan understood what it was that held the Doctor's attention. The sad remains resembled more than ever a being that was humanoid, and perhaps once more so.

"This thing, that was of the blood that built this temple, that had faster-than-light travel once," Sanchez said, exhausted but amazed. "What was the company hoping for us to find here?"

Ryan felt a dawning feeling that they were engaged in something they had only the faintest clue of.

"I think we need to bring the remains back with us." Continued Sanchez.

With the calling of the retrieval dropship, Ryan had time to reflect. This was only his first mission with the organisation and it had been one of the toughest fights of his life. But he was too tough to quit. He felt as though he was up a stream without a paddle — alone with no map and not the faintest clue about what was awaiting him out in the darkness of space.

Trying to cheer himself up as the shadow of the dropship loomed over him, he said: "At least I'm bringing back one hell of a trophy."

Sanchez could not tear his eyes away from the ruined corpse. "How could this happen?"

Ryan paused, examining the small smoking stub of what remained of his cigar, before throwing it into a pool of the things' blue blood, where it fizzled.

"He wasn't smart enough."

Well our hero Mr. Ryan is certainly one tough cookie, isn't he gunthlings? He has the holy, golden sand of Rathmar in his arteries, as my granny used to say. You know, Ramek has a similar story, when he went on a frodil hunt in the granite plains. A frodil is a kind of mutant which the machines fitted with an electronic brain, very dangerous and...

What am I relating this to you for? This is inappropriate, do not waste my time!

I am dreaming:
The Girl

Rick Damer

Long hair drags across my clean shaven face and the scent of her perfume mixes with the clean linen in my nostrils.

Ambrosia. There is no need to open my eyes as I can easily locate her, pressing up from the soft feather pillow into her full, parted lips. Wet and warm is her kiss and she bears her weight down into mine her breasts heaving against me. At first it is passionate and wanting, in scale with our desires, but now it is too much. She leans into me even harder, her bones on my bones, and my tightly closed lips save my teeth from hers and in panic my eyes shoot open to reveal the dead white eyes of the blonde and bare chested corpse from days before and as she bites into my face with her broken teeth she dissipates with the echoes of my screams. I am startled awake in the light of a new day panting and slick with sweat, white knuckling the rusted and blued revolver. My screams echo back to me off the ruinous surroundings.

I roll onto my side to take in the day and to shake this unsettling nightmare. The red morning sun casts long ruby hued shadows that run along the ruined boulevard like broken slats in a fence, etching the shades of a torn cityscape across its crowded but empty streets, streets filled with the charred remnants of a traffic jam, all urgency departed and all destinations forgotten. These same scarlet sunbeams splay across my sweaty and addled brow within my hidden raised respite.

My perch is a burnt out second-story floor, not easily accessible from the street below. A sullen sanctuary that could only be reached with the last remnants of my strength, after days of winding journeying through a hellscape of horror. Everything was burnt away and death was all I would find, until now.

When my heart rate and breathing normalize I fumble through my dwindling supplies and find a dented half-eaten can. I tear into its contents contemplating my plan of action with every bite, gripping the can tightly to muffle the scrapes of my spoon. The edge of the city is rapidly approaching, my nest rests very near its borders and the spire I awoke to days before is now a blip on the horizon behind me.

Surprisingly I have not met another creature, although there have been signs that I am not alone among the dead and the debris. The most alarming omen being the remains of a flayed man found the day before, the efficiency of the butchering has me more concerned about the living than the monsters I met in the high rise. The head and skin had been cleanly removed and were piled with the entrails in the corner of a gutted storefront- sans kidneys, heart, and liver. Cooked bones gnawed clean of flesh were scattered about the smoldering ashes of a wretched campfire, some crushed for the marrow. My stomach had turned at the dawning realization that my nose and appetite lead me there to the cannibal cuisine. I fled as quickly and quietly as I had came.

My chewing slows and the contents of my canned breakfast become hard to swallow as I relive the experience. I shudder.

I still cannot recall who I am or what led to this, and I am left with nothing but questions where a life and purpose are supposed to be. At this point the 'Where am I going?' outweighs the 'Where was I going?'. For now, it was the only question I had an answer for.

Away is where i'm going.

I slake my thirst and wash the remnants of the greasy can down with a sip from the water bladder. Suddenly the silence that had enveloped me since waking from my nightmare is broken with a clear rumble from the direction I had been heading. Then a distant crash. My eyes widen.

Then another.

A diesel engine approaches. I freeze — from my perch the remnants of the ruined street carries the clatter of the loudly tuned engine humming away at a cool timbre. Deep and breathy its droning distorted as the sound bounces along the decrepit boulevard with its mechanical cacophony, punctuated with the crashing of heavy metal. This is the only sound in all directions, the wind ceases to blow. The very world seems to hold its breath along with me as the engine approaches. Time has stopped.

Gaining courage, or relishing in my stupidity, I crawl forward to peek toward the sound, as the reeling crunch of metal reverberates and I shudder again, the chain around my neck loosing a dull rattle, my shoulders hunching to my ears. In the span of a few city blocks away, a hulk of rusted metal rolls towards me, a crude blade-like plow tossing the frames of torched roadsters violently aside with the crunching of twisted metal. Above the bladed cow-catcher the obscured window of a cab is covered in burlap obscuring the drivers, and above that twin exhaust stacks bellowing black sooty smoke into the ruddy, oily air.

The two plumes join to form a black umbilical that trails behind over a canvas and tarpaulin mosaic, tightly stretched over a trailer pulled behind the armored semi-truck. It pushes forward, closer, into the thicker remnants of the ceased traffic, tossing cars aside like empty food tins while losing no momentum. Some roll ahead and over the mess, to be pressed aside later. Others cleave in half, their mechanical guts exploding into an array of dust and bolts. Everything moves out of its way with a surreal screech of sheared steel above the droning diesel motor.

I grip the revolver more tightly and duck down to the sill, my unbelieving eyes fixed on the approaching hulk, a tractor trailer truck behemoth modified to thrive in the wastes beyond these borders.

'Should I make myself known? What terrors await me if I stop them? What terrors await if I don't?' Before I can answer these the wrecked avenue is filled with a high-pressure blast, dust and shards of metal fill the air and I am thrown to the corner of the room.

She smiles at me through her loose brown hair and I can see her green eyes twinkling as she winks playfully. She is wreathed in white lace, draped linens, and the soft glow of morning light like a gossamer halo shines over her head and shoulders. Her slender hands rise to her flushed pink face, pressing the ivory fingers to her pursed red lips, she then splays them and blows the wet mark toward me, laughing. Her giggles are like a salve to my wounded soul. Her sweet soft breath a gale of joy in my tormented tempest.

Her beaming smile then fades to a frown and she is transformed.

"Wake up", she croaks, dust billowing like a cloud from her now dry and cracked lips. Her bloodshot eyes aflame, rivulets of blood pour from her ears and nose, caking among the grime on her face. The amber hair now a muss of burnt locks and chunks of exposed and scorched scalp. Singed rags hang loose from her burnt and torn flesh as she screams,

"GET UP!"

My eyes flutter and my body stirs painfully. The girl is gone, a dream. I lay there partially concealed in the remnants of my bivouac, my body heavy and my left arm reeling in pain. The blast had removed what remained of the wall I had been hiding behind and threw me and the bricks to the back of the facade collapsed. Just beyond the ringing in my ears the sounds of muffled rapid-fire gunshots raised me from my stupor— a dream I did not want to end. The automatic weapon fire is answered in turn by a series of successive and strange 'gulps', a sound I have never heard before. Distant screams and grunts punctuate the two although no discernible words or languages can be heard. What is certain is that I no longer could hear the engine of the rig running. The explosion has disabled the road leviathan and sparked a small scale battle.

Slowly raising from the rubble, as a phoenix from the ashes, the dust pours from me. I still grip the revolver in my right hand, somehow, my left arm is mangled and hangs loosely and painfully to my side. As the dust continues to settle my view of the city is much lower than before, I am now on the ground floor, my bag nowhere in sight.

Creeping towards the chaotic combat, I hug my abdomen with my left arm, every step shaking and pulsating with the painful appendage, new pangs along my length revealing themselves with each lumbering stride.

Like a terrible trunk, a column of the super structure remains standing, providing cover and concealment from the disarray in the street. I lean heavily against it and brace myself, teeth gritting. I raise the .38 to eye level to peek into the fray, ready to fire, although I sound to be massively outgunned.

The incoming rounds now cracking past me, a flit of micro sonic booms snapping just a few feet from my aching head. The strange 'gulps' answer back, although nothing passes my position.

A quick lean to my right paints a fascinating tableau of carnage. Just a stones throw past the point of my pistol barrel the cab of the rig is still intact, the doors ajar, the hood and remnants of the engine are ruined, exploded and scattered about along with the tires torn asunder. The truck itself leans forward into a massive crater. The explosion has rent the surrounding street to an even more ruinous appearance than before. Everything has collapsed and is burning, accelerated by the fuel being carried in ruptured reserve tanks that trails behind in transport. Strange machinery fills the rest of the exposed trailer, all aflame, the tarpaulin patchwork flapping like torn bat wings in the fiery and fierce cyclone, all slowly being consumed by licking flames. An infernal tempest of dust surrounds us.

Madness. A mad world, I think, before stopping myself. *Who am I to judge this world, when I have no memory of anything, and have been seemingly born into it, fully grown, a matter of days ago? Chained to a corpse in a dead planet.*

At the precipice of the smoldering hole, flanking the ruined semi, crouch three individuals in strange attire. They are garbed in shining metal corselets, orange coveralls, and smooth metallic helmets that mask their faces,. They seem unaware of my presence. Armed with even stranger weaponry, short one-handed guns of a kind I've never seen, they fire blindly above their heads from cover. These guns produce the 'gulp' sound, and with each shot appear to carve formidable circular holes, disintegrating almost anything.

They are being fired upon by some kind of more conventional automatic weapon. Above the cover a mangled ally is splayed motionless, shot to pieces from the incoming fire just mere feet away. I can not see beyond the rear of the wreckage as the blazing hot fire sends rippling waves of distortion and heavy black smoke. The incoming rounds continue to spray, cracking past my concealment and impacting the remaining mangled vehicles in the street. Snapping along the craters rim, the automatic fire incites the strangers to stay ducked and covered.

Then I see two figures bounding closer amongst cover along the far side of the wreckage. The lead one is shooting at the strangers with an automatic rifle, the other follows closely behind. I can barely make out their features amongst the deceiving heat waves. 'Are they men?' No, one is a woman. Cautiously they creep along toward the downed stranger amid the melee.

Soon I can see, to my horror, that the two are chained at the neck with a length no longer than the one I still carry. The chain that tied me to the dead man, Roy.

Just two-arms distance away from one another they advance towards the downed foe. I watch in frozen shock as the man hands off his rifle to the girl and falls quickly on the mangled body at the front of the wreckage, ripping the strange pistol from its still hands and, firing it with that strange sound at the oddly dressed strangers who still haven't noticed me. A circular ray escapes the gun and like an invisible wrecking ball the ground cover is gouged away, in a flurry of asphalt and dust. I can see the strangers are all killed, all except one.

The woman trains the aged rifle on the crater, leaning against the wreckage for cover, but the last stranger fires on the man— the circular ray disintegrates most of the man, and launches what remains into the air, his anchored partner thrown off her feet, neck first, twisting and spinning after him like a human bola.

Snapping out of my shock at the strange events unfolding before me I train the barrel of my .38 on the gleaming helmet of the remaining stranger. My other hand feels the chain still hanging from my neck as I aim.

I have decided who my allies are.

I squeeze the trigger and the pistol bucks in my grip with the sound of ringing steel pinging in the air, the first round not penetrating the metallic helmet but glancing off and betraying my location. The armored head snaps toward me and we lock stares as the blaster is turned toward me and my eyes widen in terror, behind the blue-glass visor is the dead face of what was once a man. Opaque lifeless orbs above a frozen grimace with broken and missing teeth glare mockingly back into mine. We both fire, my shot ringing out a moment before the 'GULP' that sends forth a conical concussion, casting me into darkness.

I stand in a black room filled with darkness. Crimson light peers under and around the door frame and I yearn to leave the blinding dark.

I walk toward the door, all of my pains gone, but it does not get any closer. Each step maintains the distance, just beyond an arms reach away. I feel like my own self is in the light, the thoughts and memories I can't find...

I run, straining to feel for the exit. Then a shadow appears suddenly, breaking the sanguine borders cast by the external light. The jiggle of a knob sounds and a lump in my throat forms. The door opens and the light is more blinding and terrible than the dark.

I open my eyes for real then, to see the face and gaping maw of the stranger above me, roaring and descending to tear at my face with its broken teeth, the steely grip holding my collared chain. His helmet is gone and the creature seems to have reverted to its hungering nature as I am frozen and broken lying among the rubble.

With my inescapable fate sealed, I await to be devoured by the walker to end my living nightmare. As I prepare to succumb a shot rings out and the creature's head explodes in a gory maelstrom, coating my exposed face with viscera as the body collapses onto me.

How many times will I cheat death today?

I'm unable to move, whether broken or just held in place by rubble I do not know, or care. I'm exhausted in both thought and action, the days events being more harrowing than my descent from the tower days before. I am the only creature in the universe, born with thoughts but no memory of anything. Born to suffer.

Amidst the crunching of steps there is a scraping of something being dragged on the ground I can hardly turn my head towards the sound, but when I do I see the woman, close up now.

She is a green-eyed brunette, like the one in my dream, rifle at the ready cocked under one arm, while the other drags the lifeless torso of the man. As we lock eyes she drops her partner with a thud and the chain rattles.

"You came back." She shakes her head disapprovingly, disbelievingly.

"You stupid bastard, you came back?"

What is going on with this strange man who has no memory? Does the past live within him, or does he exist only in the moment? Where in the timeline does this strange apocalypse Earth take place? Before or after the machine wars? Stay tuned to Aegeon to find out, flower-slugs.
-Ramek

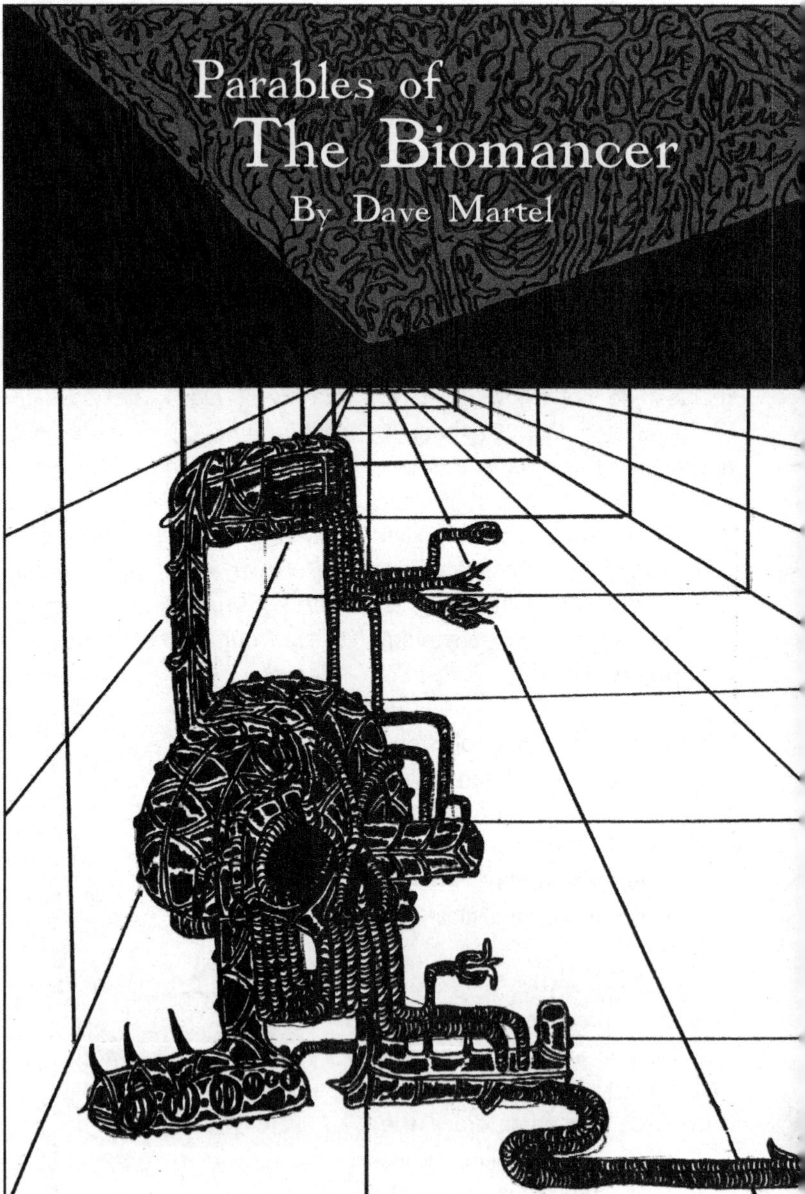
Parables of
The Biomancer
By Dave Martel

For centuries mankind wallowed in their own puddle of anxiety. Perplexed by the looming consequences of their own design. Before I enlightened them, these self-anointed apes couldn't seem to conjure the basic logic to claw their way out from their terminal descent of cyclical failure. Scarcity of resources leading to suffering then a technological solution consuming evermore resources leading to more scarcity and more suffering. Their infatuation with polymer and steel, oil and lumber. All of which draining an already emaciated earth, to which they puked the vile byproducts back into her bosom, poisoning her. Despite the fetishes of transhumanist technophiles, the solution always has been under mankind's nose. There is a resource far more abundant, accessible and renewable than petroleum, plastics, or hemp. It is a resource that has liberated us from archaic circuit boards and simplistic scripts and neural networks.

You see, technophiles have always fantasized about a singularity. A point where man merged with machine into some metamechanical apotheosis. Transcending his form and lowly quasi-conscious state into godlike awareness and existence. Despite appearing in opposition to theists of old, they both shared man's pathetic presupposition that there is a supranatural state of being for either Gods or man. I have humbled them both.

The tech-fetishists' folly was that their petty dreams were hamstrung by the resources and scarcity they aimed to escape. Foolishly believing they could liberate themselves from this techno-samsara using the very chains that imprisoned them. And as time went on they became more fanatical as their endeavors brought only more societal retardation and decay. They dreamed of an enlightened utopia but only seemed to muster more trinkets to satisfy their carnal thirsts. The higher the tech, the more lowly and bestial they became. Within a prison constructed of their own ill-begotten hubris they protested by rattling their shackles ever louder. But with every cry their manacles tightened and the more delusional they became.

It was I who saved them from their own misery. It was I who

offered them salvation.

There never was a possible merger with machines. This concept within itself is a paradox. An amusingly unsolvable conundrum. Man could never merge with machine for he was already a machine. There was no exterior resource required to fuel the biomechanical revolution for there was a resource that was more sculptable, renewable and versatile than any we have seen before. Not only was this material exceedingly abundant, we had it in excess.

Flesh.

Organic matter and its countless preassembled forms. Enamel of bones and teeth proved superior to concrete, lumber and plastics. Robotics were easily overtaken by general biomechanics, human limbs and their exquisite articulation could complete fine motor tasks far better than any hamfisted hydraulics. And finally, the fumbled attempts at quantum computing paled in comparison to the computational power of the human brain.

Technology had always been marching towards this final culmination. Not a merger of man and machine but the epiphany that man is machine. The final disregard of his antiquated moral obstacles. Morals they abandoned æons before, but continued to regurgitate, a facade hiding their ego. In ages past I would have been burned alive for commodifying the human body. While unenlightened, at least those primitive peoples had conviction.

The humanists of the subsequent postindustrial ages abandoned this belief that man's form is of divine construction and placed their own condition upon the throne of God as their highest ideal. A most fortuitous ideological development as their insincerity was easily subverted. It didn't take long for them to accept that the human body holds no sacred qualities and we are obligated to harvest it at will. Flesh is a resource as any other. Their concern was simply free access to pleasure and status. A few bribes of comfort and by sunrise the technophiles were willing biomechanical revolutionaries.

In contrast, theists proved much more stubborn. Despite the abject degeneration of their held superstitions from olden times, they clung to these superstitions nonetheless. Although naive, this stout opposition in favor of their last shreds of belief was commendable to some extent. The last pure bastion of primeval man. The steadfast conquering spirit of the ancient world. And like their ancestors before they had to be broken and demoralized.

To prove the supremacy of my innovations I genetically assembled all of their prophets. I paraded them through the streets and watched as the believers rejoiced. Hurling themselves at the feet of my creations like bewildered lambs. Christ, Buddha, Mohammed, Zoroaster and others. In the flesh, walking among them. Mindless golems of my construction.

Where I was born and the mundane details of my early life are of little significance. However, the initial thrusts towards the biomechanical revolution started at University. Before my work came to be the building blocks of civilization itself, we still lived in urban sprawls of cold concrete and steel. A fetid waste pit of smog and filth. At that time the field of science was still awkwardly attempting to break through into hyperreality with what they called "Dreamware". Cybernetic implants designed to integrate virtual space with the quackery of "consciousness". A fantastical concept of man's brain having a metaphysical element first expounded upon by phenomenologists of previous centuries. I've always found philosophy to be a masturbatory fiction of those with no other applicable skills. Nonetheless, I was forced into these dull experiments. Developing and building these foul little contraptions for hours on end. Soldering, aligning and staring through the magniscope until my eyes strained. Handling these microchips and circuits of silicone and metal disgusted me. I did not fathom the reason yet but I had an innate and visceral revulsion at these inorganic pieces of scrap.

The results of this series of experimentation were fruitless at best and catastrophic at worst, frying the subject's mind leaving them a drooling mongoloid. I pontificated on how wasting such a powerful component like the brain in favor of toyish

"Dreamware" was the exact folly that kept man in this cycle of utter failure. A cycle that needed to be shattered into thousands of unrecognizable shards. The most important lesson from this "Dreamware" debacle was about the ethics of science or lack thereof. Each of the subjects who met a painful end at the hands of these fools were shipped to the cryochamber. Their deaths covered up by university administration and their bodies filed away to hide their crimes. Despite these accidents, the experiments continued. The allure of profit and glory for a scientific breakthrough were well worth the pile of corpses left in its wake. The dean and faculty couldn't wait to pocket the checks that poured in from corporate interests.

Regardless I pressed on with my pursuits, staying in the laboratory long into the night. The frozen corpses of deceased subjects made for optimal resource harvesting. My first innovation in biomechanics was an articulating arm. I clumsily sawed the appendage from the subject and fastened it to a base. I then used oscillating electric shocks to stimulate the muscles. At first it was unwieldy with involuntary jerks and spasms. But over time I perfected it, producing a controlled appendage with the capacity of fine articulation. My obstacle was the onset of putrefaction. After several days each arm would begin emitting a foul stench making it impossible to conceal even while frozen. I then developed my first revitalization serum from stem cells and vitamin extracts. This prolonged their use but nowhere near the longevity of living flesh.

I then shifted my focus to cloning of organisms in order to maintain a fresh supply of appendages for my innovations. Various rodents and reptiles were the limit of what was available as cloning of humans was still considered unethical by bureaucratic gatekeepers and their faux moral kenning. One evening I was outraged to find my idiot dorm cohabitator was rifling through my belongings. Despite my efforts to keep my notes cryptic, he managed to decipher enough to conclude that I performed successful cloning procedures. Impressed by my prowess he continued to pry into my work. Unwilling to reveal my intention I kept my answers jovial and vague. I was unsure if he was even capable of even replicating my studies, the thought of my work being plagiarized by some slack jawed yokel was nauseating. During our conversation he made a salacious suggestion in jest that came off absurd but later became a pivotal machination in the trajectory of my destiny.

What this dullard proposed was I extract genetic samples from a female professor that he found fetching so I could then replicate her for his pleasure. Although vacuous, this scheme seemed advantageous. Being an exclusive academic institution meant there was no shortage of bourgeois fools willing to waste their inheritance to satiate their carnal hunger. I managed to harvest enough samples in her absence that proved adequate for genetic replication. My first attempt was successful but being unfamiliar with the minutiae of human gestation, I only managed to create an infant clone. Although a perfect replica, this clone was not conducive for my purpose. So, I harvested ample tissue for more procedures and disposed of the remaining subject into the rat enclosure with expectations that they would devour any remains. I was correct in this assumption

I developed adequate gestational facilities to ensure a clone could be grown to adulthood. To maximize efficiency, I performed gene therapy to accelerate the growth of the subject. Resulting in a more manageable production speed. Once again, my assumptions were correct and my experiments were once again a success. The males within my dormitory were ecstatic at my newest innovation.

Although wildly profitable, the cloned subject had little mental faculties and found her use traumatic. After some time the men found her mental state undesirable and her behavior became more erratic. To avoid detection I terminated her and disposed of the subject in the vermin enclosure. To avoid this problematic outcome again, I performed another series of gene therapy to reduce the functionality of the frontal lobe among other neurological adjustments. This concluded in a much more docile clone acclimated specifically for the purpose of repetitious sexual use.

The accelerated growth carried into rapid aging as well. The adult replica had roughly 5 months in her peak form before beginning to age and lose desirability. At this point I would terminate the subject and harvest it for resources to carry out my biomechanical innovations. This model of seamless vertical integration made for optimal production of both funding and organic material. After several years without obstacles the administration caught wind of my activities through the electronic means that I managed my wealth. I was expelled from the university for breaking the rules that they so willingly ignored years prior. In exchange for my wealth, I offered to not expose them to the authorities for their Dreamware conspiracy. An offer they accepted and an offer I later reneged. For their hypocrisy I relinquished to federal agencies copies of evidence that I kept an immaculate account of. The Dreamware scandal was a media circus that resulted in multiple arrests and executions. No retaliation against me ever occurred.

Using my model of profit and production with clones of famous actresses and performers, I managed to construct a laboratory that dwarfed the facilities I used previously. As time passed my innovations became more and more sophisticated. I eventually automated much of my operations with articulating limbs and various other organic apparatuses. Until once again I unfurled possibly my most potent discovery. "Orgrowth" or as the plebeians have aptly dubbed it "skin moss". A self maintained organic spatial cover that expands and heals, subsuming any rogue appendages in its fleshy network. I spliced human flesh with genetic matter from fungal growth to create a building material that transforms entire buildings into living structures that cost nothing and never need repair. Under their superficial growth forms various nervous systems and sinews that emulate the function of power lines, plumbing and closed circuit networks. Networks that branch out towards each other connecting on their own volition.

This allowed me to introduce ever more sophisticated organic biomechanics. Arms, limbs and appendages that articulate and perform basic tasks. Eyes and ears that act as surveillance and communication biotech. Nasal organs and lungs to detect noxious fumes and purify the air from centuries of pollution.

Orgrowth is both a civilizational and ecological marvel.

Now entire urban centers are constructed entirely from enamel and orgrowth. Articulating arms aid the elderly, automate all labor and the collapse of industry has made for a cleaner more ethical human existence in harmony with nature. The introduction of brains into the orgrowth infrastructure has made our living cities even more efficient as all things are calculated, organized and carried out without the meddling of humanity.

My final innovation will usher in a new age. Yet another transformative evolution towards the end goal of the biomechanical revolution. Not just for a single city, technology or even just humanity — but for the entirety of the planet. My final innovation is to integrate myself into the orgrowth superstructure as it spreads to eventually cover every inch of Earth's surface. The biomechanical network will be at the command of a central mind.

My mind.

As it was always supposed to be. The earth will be my body, an unfathomable organic amalgamate of millions of appendages, eyes and ears controlling all of the planet in harmonious unity. This is the final nail in the coffin for the technophiles and transhumanists. There is only to be one man to ascend to Godhood. My organic apotheosis is the finale of the biomechanical revolution. Through my genius I have made their science obsolete, their industry obsolete, their philosophies and morals obsolete.

Now the biomechanical revolution has made the totality of humanity obsolete.

Horrific! A truly twisted tale. So many ways for things to go badly for earthlings. So many pitfalls, so many doors all leading to alternate dooms!

What's my job? Turning Weaklings into MEN!

– The Golden One

REMEMBER ME? THE ONE YOU CALLED SKINNY?
POW!
OH JACK! YOU'RE A REAL MAN

LEGIO GLORIA

https://www.legiogloria.com

https://thegoldenone.se

Getting continuously stronger is the key to getting more muscular. Making small increases every week for a long period of time will eventually add up to a lot of accumulated strength. Your goal in the gym should always be to increase the weights you use, or alternatively increase the amount of repetitions you can do with a certain weight.

Patriarch:
The Golem

By James Bratton

The knights marched over a long stretch of verdant plain dotted with immense patches of fern which thrived in the dimly lit upper reaches of the Chamber. And the path sloped downward so gradually that the decline was more-or-less unnoticeable underfoot. A little further on, a rushing creek interspersed with lichened boulders and mossy stones gushed from an opening in the towering face of the inner Earth, looming ever to the knights' left as they descended. Gnarled oaks grew in sparse rows along the creek and schools of colorful little fish resembling trout swam placidly in emerald pools.

On the horizon, two parallel ridges loomed over either side of a lush valley. Far out on the hilly plain between, a herd of antlered beasts resembling elk grazed placidly and the knights speculated as to their origin. They came to a fork in the creek and followed along its leftward branch until it narrowed to a glistening stream that ran through the middle of the valley. Proceeding through the shady passage, Heydrich whistled sharply to alert the men and called their attention to a hulking shape high up on the pine-spotted ridge, which bore an uncanny resemblance to ancient sketches of the Atlas Bear in tomes they'd studied as lads. Staring back at the knights for a moment, the beast turned and lumbered off into a shadowy thicket. This broke some of the lingering tension and stirred a bit of excited chatter among the knights, who quickly gathered themselves and continued on.

Coming out of the valley, the stream widened and cascaded over the rounded edges of many low rocky terraces which descended steeply like polished granite steps. Treading carefully on the drier, lichen-covered parts near the wall, the knights made their way down.

At the bottom the downward slope of the path sharpened a bit as another plain sprawled before them, where sporadic craters marked the earth. Within their blackened pits lay iridescent chunks of obsidian-like rock which seemed to emit a dull glow, and over which the air seemed to dance like heat devils on the grassy plain. On the horizon rose a wide tree-topped plateau which loomed over a patch of thick forest that spanned the width of the path to the bottom of the Chamber and blocked their view of the other side. Pausing for a second, Wilhelm turned to the men and spoke: "We'll head to the top."

Hiking up the rocky escarpment along a narrow, winding trail; the knights crouched among the trees at the top, which blocked them from view as they looked out over the forest below. Where the tree line began, the ground flattened out into an immense shelf - comprised mostly of dense forest - and protruded further out over the chasm at the Chamber's center than any point the knights had previously trodden.

But out in a wide swathe of cleared forest near the middle sat a peculiar village, seemingly built around the entrance of a mine carved into the rock wall of the Earth. The carven lintel spanning the entrance bore hieroglyphs depicting a cube - inlaid with luminescent black jewels - hurtling through the Earth's crust in the wake of the damage caused by an immense meteor. And above the entrance loomed a deep rift in the Earth's wall, through which the furtive gleam of iridescent rock flickered in the glow of some light source within the bowels of the mine.

Leading out of the mine were steel tracks which stretched past a two-story brick warehouse. And at the end sat a riveted iron cart full of freshly-mined ore, which shimmered in the pale sunlight with an incandescent glow. And - strangest of all - a bulbous statue of similar coloration to the ore in the cart was positioned in a carven alcove next to the mine's entrance, from whose hulking shape jutted multiple spindly appendages, although the details were unclear from so far away. On the opposite side of the entrance, an identical carven alcove sat empty.

"Perhaps they worship demons", theorized Martin, to several nods of agreement.

The little straw-thatched red brick houses nearby lay in neat, gridded rows with fenced-off square sections of yard in the back, typically grouped around wells or communal ponds fed and stocked with fish by the glittering brook that snaked its way through the village, winding under networks of bridges crafted from rich-colored wood or thin slabs of cut stone. Other more eccentric dwellings sat nestled in little clearings dotted about the forested periphery of the village or perched among wooded ridges near the wall.

On the far end of the village sprawled a section of cultivated field, walled off by low rock partitions that separated individual square plots filled with familiar-looking crops like wheat and beans. In other plots grew exotic looking plants that the knights didn't recognize.

And back toward the plateau - in a little clearing in the woods outside the village - grayish plumes of smoke puffed skyward from the chimney of a little building whose roof was barely visible from the knights' present vantage point. Wilhelm thought for a moment and made up his mind.

"Hang back here, lads. We'll scout ahead", said Wilhelm, motioning toward Reinhardt, who unslung his pack and began rummaging around inside. "But Captain" Otto reasoned, seated on the gnarled trunk of a fallen juniper. "Why don't Oleg and I go in your stead. Who knows what devilry haunts these woods."

"No" replied Wilhelm, unslinging his pack. "I'll see if I can't have a talk with the fellow in that cabin before we barge into the village and cause too much of a commotion."

"We'll wave you on if the coast is clear", added Reinhardt.

Wilhelm and Reinhardt cut through the woods toward the village - staying off the beaten path - and trekked cautiously over the dense blanket of pine needles and dry leaves. Further on, a carpet of vibrant green clover covered the forest floor beneath the sprawling branches of towering redwoods. They soon reached a sharp drop-off where a crystalline stream carved its way through a gully of red clay, snaking closer to the Wall and the clearing they'd spotted from the plateau.

The knights moved further down, near a stand of trees where they could grab hold of thick roots protruding from the steep bank and ease their way down. From there they walked near soundlessly over rocks and upon a narrow shelf of clay alongside the gently babbling stream, until a break in the tree line along the crest of the ravine revealed - on the far side of the clearing near the towering wall of the inner Earth - the roof of a red brick edifice with a smoking chimney.

The knights stuck close to the wall of the gully and kept low - moving to where the bank was low enough to climb out - and peered over the top.

In front of the forge, the figure of a stout-limbed blacksmith who - standing only a little taller than the waist of any one of the knights - pounded away at his anvil like a miniature Hephaestus, his mane of braided golden hair shining in the backlit glow of the forge, amid showers of tiny red sparks. Studying his weathered, bearded face with deep wrinkles around the eyes and streaks of gray hair; the knights couldn't help but notice how his distinctly Germanic features resembled their own.

"That fellow looks friendly enough" reasoned Wilhelm, keeping his voice low. "Let's have a talk with him."

"Aye", said Reinhardt, getting ready to creep up over the bank.

The knights - still partially hidden - moved past a row of tall, purple-stemmed plants whose serrated leaves bore fragrant light-green buds, sticky and coated in sugar-like trichomes with fine red hair. They stepped into the clearing.

Looking up from his work, the blacksmith startled at the hulking knights' approach and brandished his hammer threateningly - in a defensive posture - while simultaneously inching back toward a nearby workbench whose hidden compartment bore a long, whetted knife. After a moment, he detected a certain friendliness in the demeanor of the knights and abandoned the knife. His arm shot out in a crisp Roman salute. Across the clearing, Wilhelm instinctively returned the gesture with Reinhardt following suit.

The blacksmith spoke in a tongue incomprehensible to Reinhardt but - at the same time - vaguely familiar. Meanwhile - much to Reinhardt's amazement - Wilhelm deciphered each word as if spoken in fluent German.

"No one has descended from the high wood in a very long time", said the blacksmith, bewildered. "Art thou heralds of the Old Gods?"

"Perhaps", mused Wilhelm, not quite understanding. "But it appears we've lost our way. I am Wilhelm and this is Reinhardt. We are knights of the Teutonic Order" he announced proudly. Meanwhile, Reinhardt stood awestruck at the indecipherable and seemingly miraculous exchange taking place between the two strangers, with Wilhelm apparently speaking in tongues.

"And I am Wayland, master blacksmith of Saturn's Reach" he replied, inspecting the crosses on the knights' tunics as he wiped his hands on the soot-stained apron. "Did you come from beyond the firmament?" "Yes", said Wilhelm, glancing up at the rock dome high overhead. "I suppose so".

Wayland thought for a moment. "Legends tell of a single mighty sun in a sky outside the dome, but those that dwell here mostly think such tales mere fantasy." Just about that time, he noticed Wilhelm's gauntlet. "What have you there, lad?" He inquired, sidling up to Wilhelm as he removed a hand-cut monocle from his apron pocket and lodged it securely over his right eye with a furrowed brow. Wayland's blue eyes lit up as he inspected the gauntlet. "This must be the handiwork of the Old Gods, the likes of which haven't been built in ages. And you two, as well. No one living has ever seen the likes of you this high up the road."

"Tell us, friend", said Wilhelm. "What is this place?"

"All you see", Wayland said, gesturing broadly at the wall of the inner Earth curving high up over the forge, "lies within Helios Prime, a world carved from solid rock by our ancestors, a thousand years before the oldest known civilization left their mark on the Earth. The shelf on which we stand is but one of many, interconnected along a branching path which descends toward our capitol, New Agartha. The cube at the bottom is a vessel cast down from the beyond stars, eons ago. It now rests in the pit below the city, incubating the Demiurge who corrupts living beings with its demonic energy. And whose cults terraform our world for their master's eventual birth."

Wayland continued. "And just through these woods, my home - a village once called Apollo's Reach - surrounds the entrance to a great mine, leading up toward where the first of the meteors hurled by the celestial demon sits lodged in the firmament. Our forebears once mined orichalcum from the immense rock, but the Cult of the Rat holds power here now. They've controlled the mine since I was a young lad." Lodged in the firmament, thought Wilhelm. If that's so, then the meteor must be buried deep beneath the sands of the Desert. He gathered himself. "The Cult of the Rat?" Wilhelm probed, thunderstruck by the blacksmith's words.

"Aye, the ones who worship the Cube. A race of bipedal rats who lived in the Earth before our ancestors carved out the world with their great machines. When the Cube landed, it sat dormant for a long time, but then something inside began to stir and its demonic vapors wafted up though the chasm and breathed a sort of intelligence into the already clever rat-men. Soon, their cunning grew and they began to worship a horned god in the forest who lent them dark power."

"What have they done with this power?" pressed Wilhelm, a cold feeling in his gut.

"They created golems to enslave us and keep us locked away on this side of the forest, mining ore from the husk of the meteor", Wayland said. "Though there isn't much left anymore and I shudder to think what they'll do with us when the mine runs out."

He continued. "When the ratmen were first spotted setting up a sort of camp in the Eastern Wood, they feared us and kept their distance. But they began to encroach on the village, stealing food and bits of meteorite that used to lay scattered about near the Wall. And when night fell on the sixth day, a child had gone missing. The men of the village - my father and I included - gathered our weapons and departed as a band toward the deep wood encampment, where the cult was thought to dwell. Arriving, we were shocked and unsettled to find a temple of pure white limestone where there previously had been no trace."

Wayland continued. "We made our way past crudely-assembled wooden structures and large man-sized burrows which disappeared underground and congregated silently outside the temple's entrance, where a sort of muffled, high-pitched chanting could be heard through the heavy wooden door. As we burst in, flames leapt skyward from a graven altar in the back, where burnt offerings sizzled in the belly of a horned rat carved from bronze. The rising fire cast a demonic glow over the glassy-eyed rat-men and their yellow blood-slick teeth, gathered round a sort of iron cauldron near the center of the temple, etched in strange lettering and occult hieroglyphs."

Wayland paused for a moment as he recalled the horror and continued. "And from the cauldron sprouted eight segmented legs, through ports carved in the side. Covered partially in hairs that stuck out like spines, the legs were bent, with knobbed joints extending above the cauldron's rim and plated in iridescent black metal. And at the end of each leg was an articulated claw."

"And bulging over the rim of the cauldron was a pulsating mound of brownish flesh - bumpy and toadlike - which before our very eyes burst loose from its amniotic sac with a wet pop. Fat and dark greenish fluid spilled over the rim of the cauldron and the upper torso of a vaguely humanoid monstrosity appeared, with a bulging head like that of a frog. Sunk deep in the sockets were beady black eyes. And a row of sharp little teeth lined the wide, bulbous lips that curled around either side of the head. Four fat-but-powerful arms groped madly at the putrid afterbirth encasing its grotesque form. Our party froze in fear."

Wilhelm stood in rapt attention, as Reinhardt continued to observe the conversation in bewildered fascination, discerning what he could from the pair's mannerisms.

"Scuttling toward us with a jolt", Wayland continued. "The abomination overtook our party quickly, stabbing and disemboweling the men in front with its razor-tipped legs and pedipalps, whose plating deflected whatever meager blows landed by our swords and axes. Others the golem snatched up with its four powerful arms, tearing them limb-from-limb as it laughed with a deep guttural hiss." He paused for a moment. "My father was among those slain in the Temple."

Wilhelm's heart sank.

Regaining his composure, Wayland continued. "Those who survived the onslaught turned and ran, scattering through the woods. Daring not to look back, we ran the rest of the way home, stumbling through the dark wood, silent but for the tortured screams of our comrades echoing in the night."

"Back at the village, we barricaded ourselves in the longhouse with our womenfolk and the little children who were already taking shelter there, and all through the long night we could hear and feel the scuttling of the golem as it probed about the perimeter for openings. When the sun rose and the sounds of the golem ceased, a scout snuck about the village through use of an underground passage. He discovered it empty. And nailed to the longhouse door was a letter written in blood on a scrap of human vellum, which outlined a number of decrees which were to immediately take effect."

The blacksmith went on to outline the decrees set forth by the cult, which are in summary as follows:

1. The name of the village (Apollo's Reach) will now be called Saturn's Reach

2. The villagers are to immediately forfeit all weapons.

3. The villagers are to mine the meteorite deposits and deliver them to the temple, by no later than sunset every sixth day.

4. The villagers must eat only plants and insects, instead of game from the forest.

5. The villagers must never pass through the woods where the Cult dwells. They must never move further along the path toward New Agartha.

"And the cult patrols the forest with their golem - of which they soon made another - and blocks the road toward New Agartha and everything in-between. All living in the village were born here and know no other way" Wayland finished.

"I see" replied Wilhelm, having already made up his mind. "It appears we share a common foe, as I seek passage through the cult-haunted woods, toward New Agartha. I have under my command a dozen of the strongest men living, atop yonder plateau", he said, pointing. "Tell me; what weapon might we forge to harm these creatures?"

"The golem's limbs are plated in sheets of forged meteorite. Steel cannot pierce nor break it. Only a weapon forged from meteorite ore can destroy another."

"Have you the ability to forge such a weapon?"

"Yes" he answered confidently. "The picks we use in the mines are forged from meteorite - and I have made a great many over the years - but they are kept under lock and key, inside the mine, and are too small to properly damage the golem's hide".

"Have you the skill to forge mace and warhammer for a fellow of that size?", Wilhelm said, pointing to Reinhardt, who fidgeted uncomfortably in confusion.

"Aye" affirmed the blacksmith, "But I'll need your help and we'll need more ovens and bigger ones. And we'll need to fetch more ore from the mine."

"Can you oversee my men in the construction of the ovens? And direct them toward the ore?"

"Aye", said the blacksmith, welling up with emotion as his eyes became bleary with tears. "I've long waited for such a time", he said. "For years I've dreamt of revenge."

"Then worry not, good blacksmith. You shall have it now."

STAY TUNED FOR PART III

Revenge is justice. Revenge is natural. Ramek understands vengeance and supports those who seek it.

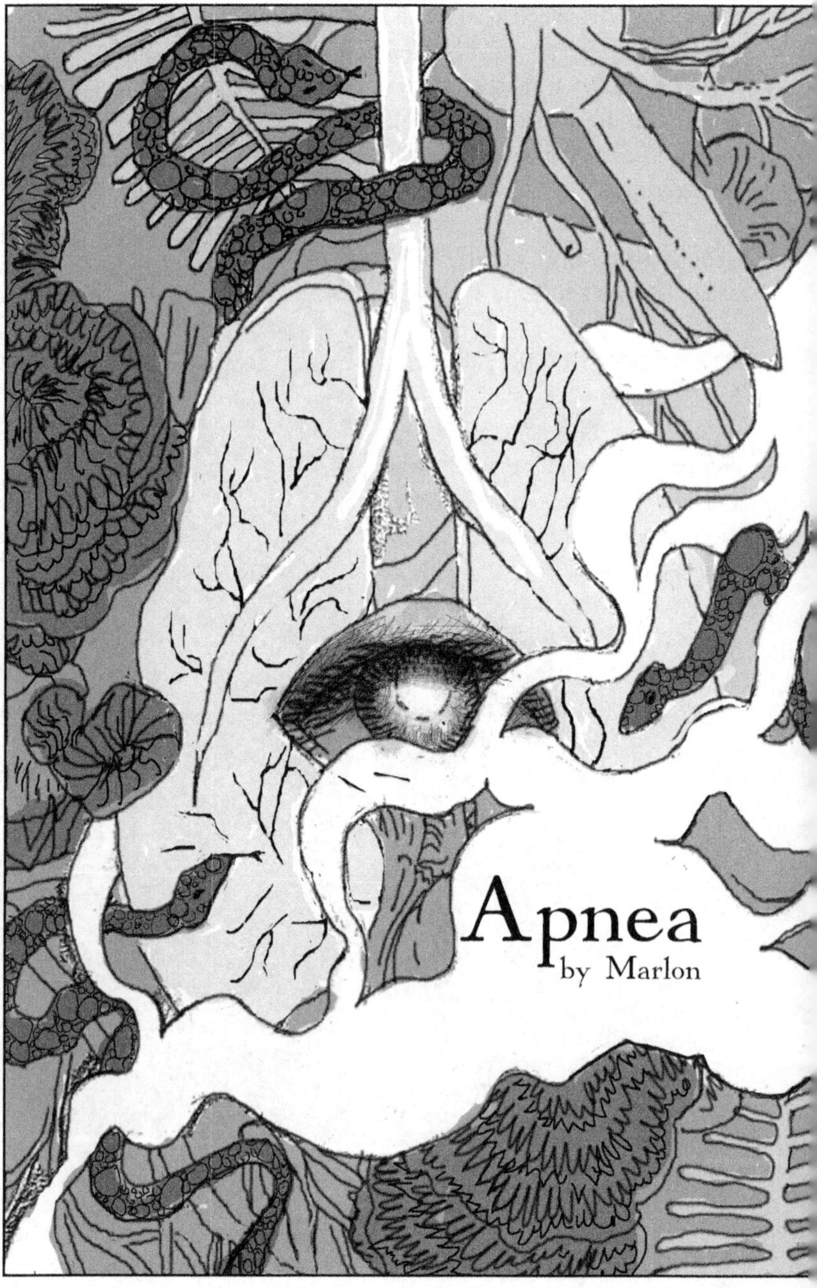
Apnea
by Marlon

The night-images began after I rejected the insufflation treatments. I was able to see where the distributors were — nearly microscopic-sized tubing in the walls, on every streetlight and protruding from tree bark. I began to hold my breath to avoid the gas.

I am writing this on a terminal I stole from Janus Industries' Faith and Freedom government adjunct office. Dreaming, and writing, is now prohibited without official sanction from the Faith and Freedom office. I know now that the office scans our REM neuronal wavelengths to suppress any dangerous, undemocratic propaganda. This, they fear, is the most dangerous risk to the continued existence of the state apparatus.

I don't recall when the night-images began, or when I came to believe that they represented reality within a chasm of the unreal — more real than what was propped up around me. I would wake up at night, every night, choking for air. I came to deduce that the medication distributor the Office had installed in the state-owned apartment I was gifted (for my safety and inoculation, I was told) was sucking all the air out of the room. I opened the window that minuscule amount sanctioned (to prevent suicides) and put my face against the glass, inhaling what little oxygen the office released into the thick night air.

I once witnessed a picture of a lung alongside a forbidden picture of a tree. The resemblance was striking. That moment was the origin-point, the same moment that I began to witness night-images during the day.

They are scanning now, I can feel that behind my eyes. I can't maintain these thoughts, I must relinquish them. They can make it difficult to breath.

I am a citizen of the Democracy. I must atone for the sins of the past. I deserve nothing and am capable of very little. I am here to build a future that benefits the Democracy. I am to report for surgery within the next three months or lose access privileges. For my safety, well-being, and mental health, I am to report for surgery.

The insufflation pipes release

steam, and the medicine fills the room. I plug them up, those I have found, with wet cloth. I have to breathe it in, I have no choice. The neoviruses will spread. A new plague variant has been discovered, its origin irrelevant, jumping species from an animal to animal and then on to humans.

The woman who takes my breath away gave me an old modified radio that can hide my signal. I turn it on, with a hiss like boiling water. I feel glass in my eye and am helpless but the pain subsides. My thoughts return, coalescing, but fragmented. I must write them down or lose them forever.

I can't sleep anymore, not really, not since I was able to deduce that I was already asleep, and so was everyone else. I would think I was awake, drinking a glass of water, but as I lowered the glass, the night stand would shift to a different corner. The light pole outside was now on the opposite side of the street. A room in my house went missing.

I must have always been dreaming.

There are forbidden bookstores, smoke-stained rooms with wallpaper depicting forgotten animals and myths — strange symmetrical bugs and creatures out of a beautiful nightmare. She took me to one, the 'Shadow Puppet' it was called, and the information in the yellow pages that smelled like dust and wood contradicted most of what is in the new books. Trees and mushrooms, the most marvelous of beings, were alive. That's when I began to see the vines and snakes alongside the pedestrian tunnel walls, flashes of fecund, dirty roots and slime and slick brown fungi growing right before my eyes, sprouting like bubbles. I scanned the eyes of others but they saw nothing, and I looked away and realized I had held my breath.

In the Office lab they kept a virile, alert terrier. They wanted to know if he dreamt and stored memory. This wasn't the real reason though, for the experiments. They removed part of his brain while he slept, just a small piece at first. He awoke from the insufflation-induced slumber and was able to recall commands. They took out another part of his brain, and he was less virile, less alert. They repeated this until there was nothing left but the stem.

"Still alive," the Office scientist said, smiling, rubbing his head.

I know this seems impossible, unimaginably cruel even, but do not be naive. The best scientists of the age sawed open primate skulls, attaching electrodes to the gray matter, deep within the tissue, to determine which region corresponded to what emotion. To this terrier they repeated the process until I lost count. In their restricted room I once saw a picture of a dog's brain and a human brain. And that's when I knew. The steam medicine — it was attenuating the brain, and the Office wanted to quantify how much could be removed and weakened while still allowing for some level of functioning.

They invoked the eternal plagues — it was always out of necessity that the measures were taken. Waxy welts and pox and nose bleeds and engorged lymph nodes. The programming was incessant, a parody of reality, the gory photos interspersed with subliminal cues. Manipulating your instincts, straight to the brain stem, the oldest region, which you cannot ignore. Your brain like a machine-gun reacting, firing off a stream of chemicals which light up the neural spiderweb, re-spinning its image so that in time it is something else entirely, unrecognizable, and you don't even remember what a tree looks like, who your master is, what it means to keep a dog, or how it feels to wake from sleep and see sunlight entering in through the glass, heating your skin.

"To prevent the extirpation of our Democracy, insufflation every hour. Janus Industries. For the future survival of our Democracy, new births must coincide with new death. The count will be tracked by the Committee on Survival and Family Planning. The Office will provide children as a gift." I was able to deduce that each child, if it was a real child, was passed on from family to family as it aged in staggered cycles, so that many families raised the same child. We were too inoculated to notice.

The intent, I believe, was to encourage certain behavior and discourage misbehavior, the soul nudged like cattle through the maze until the will is suppressed. Single file. *Don't think that. I can't remember. This is forbidden to write.* I see the vines curving down the ceiling, ferns flapping like wings, expanding and contracting in natural cadence. The insufflation sprinklers come on and they disappear, the room dark and empty but for a yellow light in the corner on top of a night stand that wasn't there.

The insufflations began. In high-traffic, congested areas, a sprinkler comes on every hour to release the treacly steam. Skepticism, never mind defiance, was met with recriminations of insolence and even murder. So we happily breathed it in, waiting for that subtle narcotic.

"We can't show you your records. Privacy, you know. You have to trust me. We care for you and it motivates and informs everything we do. You are the reason I got into this field — it wasn't the compensation or prestige. The risk of litigation alone," the doctor said, smiling without showing teeth, and patted me on the shoulder.

The Milgram experiment. That was one of the clippings she sent me. A dog is naturally obedient because they are naturally trusting, but trust is a priceless currency that must be earned. This is forbidden. I trust those that are in positions of authority because they are more intelligent and selfless and have purer motives than the average person. They are above average and have a sophisticated, highly developed, enlightened conscience. To think otherwise means the disintegration of the Democracy... I am having a forbidden thought and my eyes are bulging out of their sockets, bleeding down each tear duct.

"We removed gray matter next to the frontal lobe and the dog attacked its master. I think we should put him down."

This was a difficult one. Had the dog's conscience been removed along with his mind, or had he become conscious and acted accordingly *This thinking is forbidden and I am now nearly blind, the buzzing sound like a fly I can't see or kill. I think they interlace the circuits behind each eye at birth and that is why... I cannot go on. The thoughts are drawn out of me, and they shatter.*

"To prevent the extirpation of our Democracy, insufflation every hour. Janus Industries. The inoculation will spread through the air and, combined with an anti-viral, will protect you from the plagues. For the survival of our Democracy, new births must coincide with new death. The counts will be tracked by the Committee on Survival and Family Planning. Do not be selfish, resources are limited and we are overpopulated. The insufflation will prevent birthing. This is a temporary measure and is entirely reversible. The insufflation apparatus will be removed in two years, and then we can get back to our normal lives."

The terrier behaved in a completely normal way. They were able to remove most of his brain and he still remembered his handlers, where his bed was, where his food bowl was, when he should be fed, faces.

"Memory is like a spiderweb. The nodes are connected, but those closest to each other can trigger activation of nearby memories. It is possible that they do not reside in one place."

This was when I began to see the night-dreams during daylight, the sphere barely visible behind the everlasting clouds. I saw the ferns and roots and spiderwebs and vines crawling above me, always out of reach, in my waking hours. Spiderwebs materialized after a blink. I reached out and they vanished. I held my breath. Perhaps I was no longer sleeping.

She took me to a cave underneath a bluff overlooking a valley. There were symbols I did not recognize that led us to the cave and carved onto the rock was the word 'Prohibited'. Inside, in a small opening, was a bookcase, a gnarled tree trunk, a rusted metal brazier, and sacks. She opened a sack and pulled out a glass vial. Inside were dried, scaly mushrooms. She held my hand.

"Take these. You may lose something but gain even more. What you are capable of."

I read a note I recorded earlier: When I sleep I sometimes wake up because I stop breathing, but during the day, before the awakening, I barely exchange oxygen with the air around me and I am mostly asleep even when awake.

The insufflation steam transformed into spiderwebs, and small black spiders came out of the sprinklers along with the medicine, their compound eyes slightly aglow with azure fire. I laughed. Poor dog, he trusted them.

In the cave we promised each other we would take a flight to the farthest country possible. They still had flights, vacation getaways, if gifted, where one could witness the degeneracy of other countries, away from this Utopia. However, the rules were strict and every step along the way was controlled. There was a getaway opening in several months' time.

There were three checkpoints through security. At any point they could increase the insufflation or inject straight to a person's vein.

"Attention travelers. Security checks counterbalance the risk of the infected spreading their diseases. The Committee on Health and Wellness has approved these measures. A safe journey, freedom from infection."

She made it through with only a minor insufflation tubing. I was accosted.

"Sir, are you nervous? Look behind you sir."

I turned around and superimposed on a silhouette of my body on a glass screen were three red boxes, one on my chest, one of my hand, and one directly on top of my groin.

"Did you check your pockets, sir? I will have to check your groin, sir. Would you like me to do that here or in a private screening area?"

"That's strange. Right here is fine, please."

"Sir, are you nervous? Pull your pants up please." He passed a wand over my hands and pressed my balls with his hands. "Your eyes appear a little bloodshot, sir," he said and shone a light into my vision. I became dizzy and fought the urge to pass out.

"As nervous as one should be with a stranger's hands on their balls, sir. Yes, not much sleep last night." I felt my eyes water, with blood or tears or both.

"Ok, you know we have a pill for that. Have a good day, sir." He smiled a gray, toothy grin and patted me on the back.

We boarded the plane. The seats were configured obliquely and the backs could not recline. I knew from the Office lab that the insufflation on the plane was intended to increase blood flow, drowsiness, and suppress appetite. I lost track of where she sat. I sat. And waited. I fought the urge to fall asleep as the gas emitted from the air ducts. I could hear the slight whirring of the machines and smelled the sweet insufflation. The man next to me exclaimed with joy.

"Ah, here comes the medicine, bring me the medicine," and he took a few deep breaths, his eyes bulging in anticipation.

I awoke in darkness. The windows were all shut, and I scanned the hazy cabin and made out only a few passengers, each one a few rows ahead and behind. The insufflation was thick, making it difficult to see. I fought the drowsiness but I could barely move, and sleep seemed like the most comfortable state in the world.

"Sir, would you like a sleeping aid? Just a few more hours to go sir."

I awoke again. Outside an open porthole I saw white blurs of snow streaking diagonally against a perfect black darkness. We had landed. A yellow light far in the background shone on top of a tubular gray structure. I looked around me. The cabin was dark except for the seatbelt and no smoking sign lit up on the ceiling panel. I expected to hear furtive, somnambulant movements next to me, but instead I only heard the slushing of snow against the porthole and a wailing, whistling sound. Wind, probably. The sleet hitting the aircraft. The yellow light in the background dimmed until it was gone. There was nobody seated around me. The insufflation whirring came one. An attendant floated down the aisle.

"Excuse me, have we arrived?" I asked as she approached my aisle. I could barely make out a face in the darkness. A red light flashed against her face and I saw that she wore a black, protuberant mask.

"Calm down sir, we are stopped here as a precaution. We will be airborne shortly."

"Oh, yes, of course. Where are we, exactly?"

"Newfoundland, sir."

"Ah and where are my shipmates?" I asked cheerfully.

"We've had to distance the passengers, I hope you understand. There was a risk of infection on board that was missed during screening. Our filter should clear it out, but this is just a precaution. We will be airborne again in just two hours, to allow proper time for our filters to work and for the air to cycle through. Please just sit tight and we'll be at the destination in no time." She hurried along, her face like some chimerical human anteater hybrid. Her rubber hand placed a plastic glass of water in my lap.

"Just drink this, sir."

"Yes, of course. Thank you." I didn't swallow and spit out the water on the seat next to mine. I could see a shadow moving a few seats down the aisle. Please be her, I thought. The thought of sleep was like a dream, and I wanted nothing else, even if it meant death. Her image superimposed on my vision, I held my breath and hit my face with a closed fist, but the medicine was too strong.

A chiming, like bells, woke me. The cabin was brightly lit. The panels on top of my seat slid open and those yellow masks and bags with the rubber headbands came down. I opened the porthole and saw only sleet but thicker this time and pitch black in between. The yellow light flashed, but maybe it was the wingtip lights. The plane seemed to pitch slightly. Maybe we were airborne.

"This is the captain speaking. Everyone please do not panic

and put on your masks. The pressure should equalize once you breath in. We are off the coast of Newfoundland and will reach the destination once filters have had enough time to cycle through."

Where the hell was Newfoundland? I looked around and saw a few rows in front me hands frantic for the masks, heard elastic bands snapping and quick, sharp panicked breaths. Like rabbits at the cutting board. The mask dropped in front of me. I wanted to scream her name. Maybe this was it. The insufflation whirring overpowered the wailing wind outside, I could see the gas floating out of the ducts, as thick as smoke billowing out of a forest fire. Vines, dazzling and kaleidoscopic, crept down the ceiling, ancient ferns fanned my face. They covered the ducts. I reached out but never could touch the vines, they always moved away at the last minute like fish underwater. I was half asleep, half dreaming, and my breath was slow. But I had to reach her. I moved my legs, crumbled down as if I had none. I saw a torso hanging out from his seat, tongue hanging out of his mouth on the aisle floor, eyes bulging and wide open, still breathing in the gas through the bag. An attendant saw me, and several others this time, and grabbed me by my underarms, sliding me back.

"Sir, this is an emergency, go back to your seat sir."

"What's the emergency? Are we in Newfoundland?" I gagged. They all wore the same protuberant, black rubber masks. One of the attendants righted the torso back up on his seat, his tongue still hanging out of his open mouth and his eyes white.

"We've almost reached the destination, we just need your cooperation. There's been an outbreak. The new plagues. You will be fine. The insufflation will cure you."

Or maybe, I thought, *we were brought here as undesirables, for pacification, lobotomization, or death. You are capable of so much more*

"Ah yes, I thought I felt a boil somewhere on my scalp. I will cooperate, I will not be selfish, I don't want to put anybody in danger due to my own poor hygiene."

I caught a glimpse of her face down the aisle, the spark still in her eyes. My breath left my body at the sight, visions and memories awakened from within the glistening, kaleidoscopic spiderweb my mind had woven, diamonds in the desert. And then they were gone, retrievable only if kept close to the heart, that other region somewhere along the grey matter.

The vines grabbed the attendants' wrists, pulled them away and onto the ceiling. Maybe, or maybe I was seeing what wasn't there, and they left back to their seats, leaving me to choke on the medicine. I held my breath, I fought the insufflation. I crawled to the man with his tongue hanging out. He had once again fallen over from the side of his seat, as satisfied as a junkie, his head nearly to the ground. I pulled his torso to the floor and held a plastic cup to his mouth. The breath condensed against the plastic, transforming into tiny beads. He was still breathing. I tore a plastic bag from the ceiling, my lungs burning. I could barely see my own hand, so thick was the medicine, as if the plane had cracked open, the vapor clouds outside rushing in while we remained motionless and suspended in the sky. I fashioned a two-way plastic hose with the bag, cups, and elastic bands, and placed one cup over the man's mouth and pinched his nose. I sucked in air on my end, sucking in whatever unadulterated oxygen remained in his chest cavity, a reverse resuscitation. My mind cleared, but it wasn't enough. I was dizzy and the thought of sleep still tantalized me.

I took the hose and crawled to the lavatory. I lifted the lid to the latrine and sealed as best I could one end of the hose against the opening to the waste chamber. I put the other end to my mouth and took a deep breath. It was the cleanest air I had taken in in years. The dizziness and somnolence subsided. We weren't airborne, I thought — the plane wasn't vibrating. I sucked in air again, kept the bag as a reserve, and ran down the aisle to her prostrate body.

She was alive. I grabbed as many jackets from the cabin as I could and a few bags from the bins for good measure. I opened the emergency exit and ran out into the snow. My eyes bled but their signal was too weak here. Wherever we were. The coldness and pain as I leaped onto the tarmac made me alert and I felt awake for the first time. We entered the darkness and void, gasping at the cold air, coughing up our lungs, laughing, and ran until we were out of breath.

Ramek finds this harrowing. It is like being in the man's brain. Ramek is shaken. What escape is there when one's own thoughts comprise the prison walls?

There is no escape from that gaol.

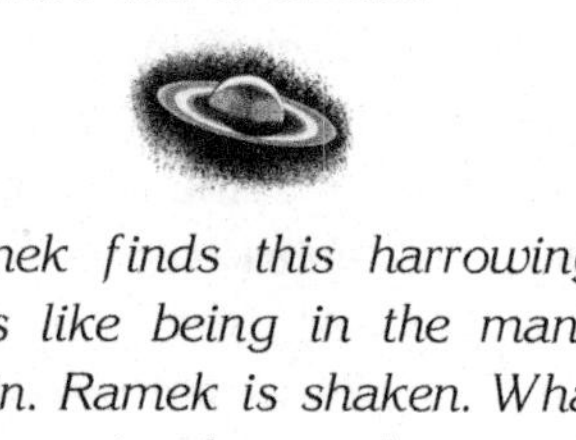

The
Bizarchives

Evolas' Dream

By Brendan Heard

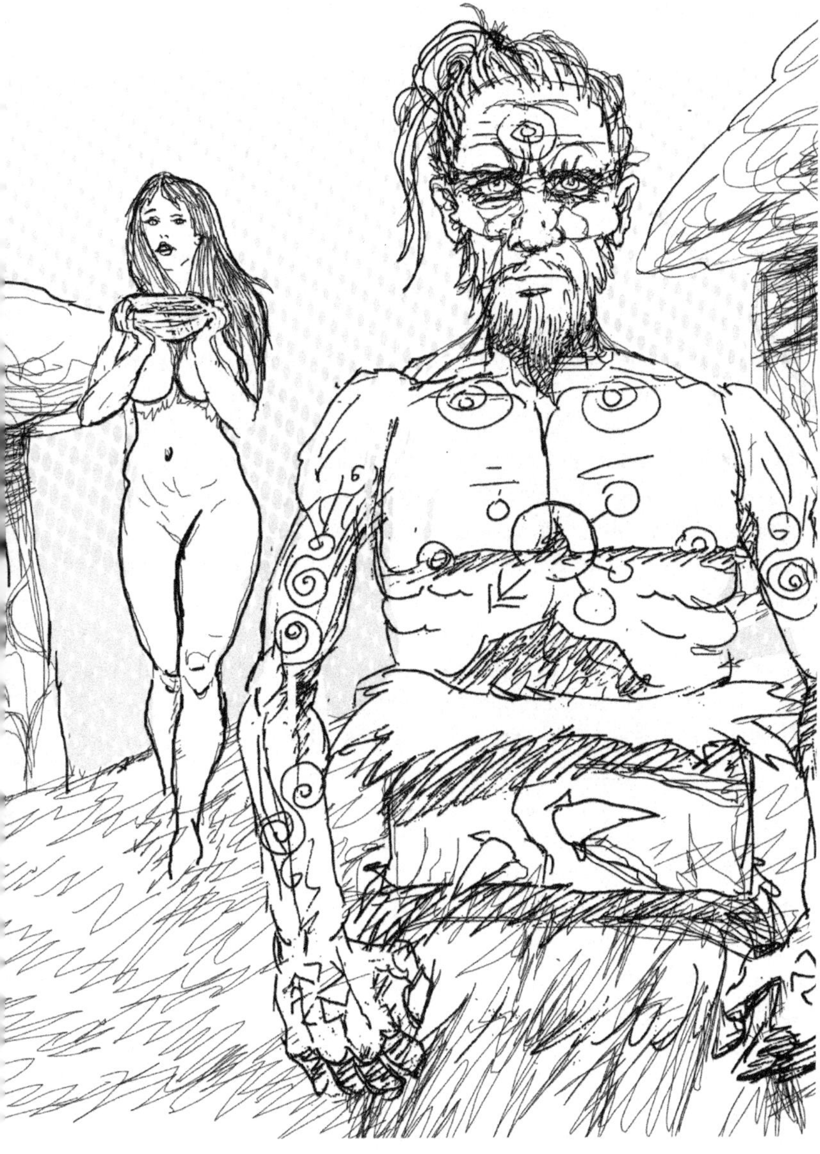

Julius Evola was wheeled by his nurse into the reading room. He was 76 years of age, and felt perpetually cold, and his irregular heartbeat prevented him from sleeping well. He felt exhausted from living.

"Grazie, Maurice." He said as the nurse gave him his medicine, and pushed the baron's wheelchair past his extensive library, and left him before a large fireplace, where two criss-crossed mortuary swords hung over the mantle.

The baron had not had a proper rest for days, however this night, sitting in his chair before the crackling fire, he fell into a deep sleep. His well-worn copy of Junger's Blätter und Steine slipped down from his plaid covering blanket, and bounced off the spokes of his wheelchair before hitting the floor. The baron did not wake, as the crackling and pops of the wood-fire droned along with his heavy breathing. Drowning out all other noise, including the irregular, strained beats of his heart — as he slipped into the unconscious.

He was receding into his mind, into the dreamscape. He was travelling, like a bird, like a released soul. He could feel a wind, or a freedom which was similar to flying, as he passed through a tunnel, mighty in its breadth, and lit up all about. He felt dizzying possibility, like his soul was freed from the earth, moving among the stars. He felt a vast and impossible chill at the prospect of the void without.

Where would he go? Would he reach the eagle plane beyond the plane of fire? But he realized then he was not exactly dead, not yet. He was not going forward in time to his own afterlife and beyond, but backward. Back before his birth.

He began to feel the cold more viciously, and while aware that he was within a kind of dream, he felt that he was waking. The tunnel reduced to a tiny size, and then to a small point of light, but as he reached this he awoke. Or he dreamed he awoke, while still within the dream.

He was no longer disembodied, nor in a tunnel of light, but in a fen of grassy hills. Ancient looking hills with long grass, grown on the same spot for centuries, blowing in the wind like ocean tides. The air was crisp, so clear and sweet, the air itself seemed full of sunlight, and Evola sensed he was in the world when she was still young. He noticed movement, and that he was surrounded by men busily working. The men were primitives dressed in animal skins, and they were busy hauling stones, great massive stones, using gargantuan prehistoric mammals. Evola recognized the unusual and massive shovel-shaped tusks of the early species of elephant, the Gomphotherium, strapped about with leather lashes and dragging a mighty menhir, guided by one of the men on its back. In a further fen he saw a group of the primitive men standing over the fallen body of a giant woolly rhino.

Evola became somewhat aware then of what they were erecting. Wooden poles surrounded the summit of the hill on which he stood. The great Gomphotherium stomped past him, grunting, so close its steamy breath washed over his head. The primitive man did not so much as glance at him, he was unseen in this dreamscape. *But I am really here?* he thought. *How is it so real?*

He stared intently at the elephant-rider. His hair was shorn except for long topknots, spooled about the side of his head in circles. He was partly naked save for skins and furs, a flint axe in his thick belt. Some kind of massive fur pelt acted as a saddle, and hanging from this, swaying beneath the giant Gomphotherium's legs were human skulls, tied to the pelt by frizzy primitive cordage.

It felt real, not like a dream. The details were intense. *Can I wake myself up?* He wondered. He dared not, he did not wish to miss any details. But he suspected that he couldn't wake himself, that he was now riding the line between life and death, that he really was witnessing an historic Neolithic event.

The man's hair was coppery, and his deep set eyes a brilliant white blue. His skull shape was unusual, the cheekbones were very prominent, almost like armour, and the man looked very thin, but big-boned and strong. Evola guessed his height was under five foot.

The giant stones were being placed outside the wooden poles. They dug up massive furrows where the beasts of burden dragged them, some of which dragged enormous logs.

As well as this, great teams of the hoary men pushed stones along on smaller logs, or pivoted them on much smaller stones. He saw too in the distance some of the men using a primitive version of a medieval crane, with logs and an extremely crude walking-wheel. *Much more advanced than history has given credit for,* he thought. *But how else could such magnificent stone architecture have been constructed?*

All this he noted, recording the details in his mind, as though he were a dream-archaeologist. At a distance he noticed then that the enormous cairn that the crane was employed in building, or series of them, resembled in many ways stonehenge, but vastly larger. The proportions were of a scale he could scarcely have imagined from such early man.

Another large prehistoric mammal roared in the distance, unseen, sounding different than the others, and he wondered what it was. Its paean carried on the wind, as the people gathered in greater numbers about the hillock. He noted that the men had not thus far spoken, had hardly uttered a sound, and worked in silence apart from grunts.

But what was the structure? What was it for? He walked up close to one of the men, getting a good look. Not unlike any pre-industrial man who had lived out-of-doors his whole life. They were caucasian of type, though almost Asiatic of cheekbone, there was a variety of eye-colour, but a truly icy, near-white blue was dominant. Hair was mostly fair, some nearly white-blonde, but many were intensely curly, even frizzy. They kept this in various styles, mostly long, with the men often shaving the sides, similar to Cossacks. The skin was leathery, browned, almost shiny, and pulled tight about the eyes, which were large and far apart.

There was a sense of pitiless fierceness about them, in a restrained but intelligent way. It was like examining a hawk at rest, you could sense it would take but a moment's change to effect a sudden lethal strike.

Evola was distracted from his examinations then by the entrance of a very tall man in bear furs and a helm of red stag antlers of great breadth. He was led in a procession upon pall bearers, with two naked young women who were led at the front, tied at the neck by leather straps. They were coloured over with wode or tattoos, he could not immediately tell, and were quite beautiful for women of this wild type. Evola sensed they were virgins, and that a rite was going to take place to commemorate the building of the structure. Whatever it was. The man was singing, the first evidence he had of language. It was very unusual, especially how it was sung, which resembled a cross between Celtic-Iberian folk and Mongolian throat whistling. Of the words he could not sense any relation to any language he knew, not immediately. He did feel moved by the music, which hit an emotional pattern and resonance he had never quite heard before. A very young man from the crowd began to accompany the old man on a strange bone flute of some sort.

He sensed a light change and looked up and saw that the sun was beginning to set, and a brilliant night sky was slowly opening up, though partially obscured by clouds. The surrounding hills boiled away at the edges in a violet orange, and he saw an eagle flying past, circling, slightly to the east. The tall man pointed to this, and the two virgins knelt.

The procession began to light torches, and the stones which had been dragged out by the heavy animals were unlinked from their dragging harness. The massive creatures were led to an outer periphery, where they circled the inner group of humans, as the tall man and his priestly entourage entered the inner stave circle in which Evola noticed a large ground-level slab of ancient stone, which had been partially obscured by long grass and wild flowers. He could see now, examining it, that there were concentric circles carved crudely into it.

The virgins were given large stone cups, full of amber fluid, some kind of psychedelic, Evola guessed. His mind was busy recording all the details. He moved about them completely unseen, counting the stones that had been dragged in.

Eleven in total.

They were unmarked, similar in size, and he saw holes had been dug where they were to be placed, vertically along their length.

How would they raise them, he mused, *the animals again? The crane? Balancing and pivoting them on smaller stones?*

He saw they had impressive rope and tether systems, some of their wood beams had intricate carvings, some were shaped to a medieval level of geometry. There was plenty of evidence of stone carving and stone tools everywhere, and he stopped to examine a warrior who walked past then, the sides of his head shaved, with a wheel-like tattoo on the shaved part of the scalp. The man had a flint axe proudly placed in a wide leather belt, tied with leather string over rabbit pelt breeches. The man was topless despite the cold evening air, and had more interesting tattoos Evola would have been keen to study, but there was so much to take in at once. The marks seemed esoteric, crudely executed, but some resembling symbolic significance he could almost recognise, as well as many which were unknown.

The clouds over the mound seemed to gather, and Evola realized then, despite the realism of the dream-vision, or whatever it was, that reality was altering now into the supernatural.

Directly over the knoll altar the cloud swirled quickly, into a sky-gyre, originating far up in the air, and drawing all the clouds about this in a spiral. The red of the setting sun gave this sky an apocalyptic tinge, and the old man's song became louder, and some of the warriors began to give strange hoots or shrieks, war cries, and some of the group began to grovel, and others to do a strange dance, and even the large beasts began to sway their shaggy heads and stamp the ground.

Evola felt immediately drawn to this, as a transient spirit without material in their realm, and flitting like a ghost, he moved past the gathered cultists, who were becoming frenzied at the sight of this incredible weather, and he stood upon the stone at the hill's peak, looking upward. He could see straight up the gyre, to its dark center, and saw the eagle from earlier, circling fearlessly about this.

Evola then looked down at the throng. It seemed to him then that they could see him now at last, or some sense of his form was being sensed by them, as they stared at him with bulging eyes, no longer entranced by the impossible clouds.

Evola looked to the shaman, who returned his gaze with obvious acknowledgement, his eyes wide in amazement. Evola felt a warmth at a genuine human reaction: recognition — and saw in the man's response, despite his incredibly distant genealogy, a reaction like that of any other man.

The old shaman made a sign with his hands, strangely not unlike crossing himself, and pulled a short flint dagger from inside his robes. Not guessing and not wanting to know his intent, Evola looked skyward again.

The vortex swirled and swirled, as he heard the screams of the people, and the roars of the mega-livestock, and the wind was growing stronger and the long grass of the fen sounded like hissing ocean waves. Evola reached down and took great handfuls of the cool mossy ground beneath the grass in each hand, he could not physically uproot it, but he could feel it. It occurred to him that this might be the last physical sensation he would have, disembodied as he was, and likely departing the human world, if only to be recalled on the great wheel.

Looking up again the gyre was more intense, and more red, and utterly mesmerizing, and he could no longer look away. He began to feel like he was in the tunnel of light once more, the one that had taken him from his broken old body to this place, and while he could still hear the wind in the grass and the now manic singing of the old man and the bone flute, and the panicked grunting of the prehistoric elephants and pack animals, he was already travelling. He let himself feel lifted, and his spirit seemed to rise from his dream body, which was already incorporeal. He had a feeling then, like he was leaving behind his own shade, his ghost, here in the far distant past, among these people, to haunt these Neolithic lands well into the future, and beyond. This seemed to him a fitting end.

His soul, however, would now depart. And so it did.

In his study, sleeping before his fireplace, Evola's heart ceased beating.

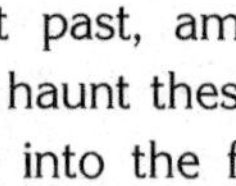

Ramek likes to think all great philosophers die in such a similar matter. Their soul or intellect is time-warped to a place where they can have a final ghostly influence, unknowable in its meaning or breadth to all but the god of time, who I know as Zazek, and who you scroats might know as Kronos.

Everyone's final journey is certainly a retreat of the soul from this plane.

Seeking human meaning in these things at all is likely fruitless, as we are too biased towards continually surviving on this plane as long as we can, to view the objective master of the Whole in its clockwork mastery.

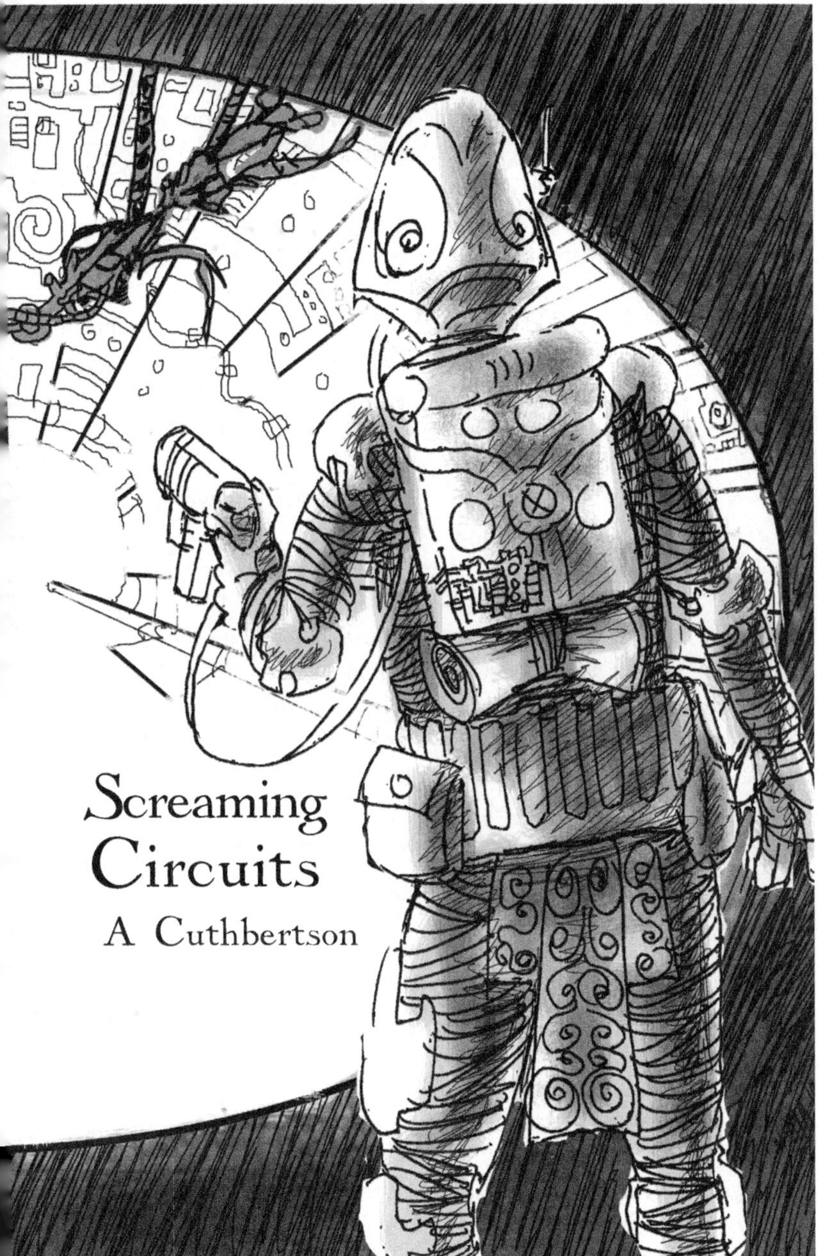

Screaming Circuits

A Cuthbertson

With an emission of steam and a flurry of sparks, the metal door slid open in front of me and revealed the pitch-black interior of the ancient spacecraft; the third we had found in as many months. My two fellow Deliverancers and I stepped out of the landing pod and shone torches warily into the dark.

We stared down a long corridor; our high-powered torches revealed a door at the far edge. Thankfully, there was nothing else of note in this passage. Walls and flooring made of ancient alloys; functional, not beautiful. Primitive, yet robust. The gravity-fields weren't active here, so we were floating, propelled gently by small boosters in our backpacks. Our scanners indicated that all was well in the rooms beyond. We would be able to walk normally once past this door; a miracle considering how long this thing had been abandoned.

This wing of the ancient craft had weathered the effects of radiation and space-debris rather well. The other parts of the ship, not so much. We'd spent a lot of the last week carefully clearing a path to this area with lasers and explosives, securing a landing spot in this corridor where the outer wall was weak enough for the landing pod to punch through.

We glided down the corridor slowly, confident, but not hurrying. It was big enough to float two-abreast, with a third behind; I ushered the pair of them out in front of me. I cared not to learn their names.

It was easier this way.

They'd been freshly awoken from cryo-sleep for this excursion, and I was prepared for a slightly wider range of contingencies than they were. I outranked them, and their fellows-in-rank had not made it back from the previous two ships we explored. In short, they were more expendable than me — and I fully planned on making it back alive. Therefore they were leading the way, and I wasn't about to get attached to them.

I kept my boltgun lowered, but ready to draw up at the first sign of danger. There hadn't been much danger to speak of in the first ship, not the kind worth shooting at anyway. But the resulting complacency had led to accidents in the second excursion, and I wasn't taking any chances this time.

In the first ship a couple of tripwire-triggered explosions had led to one of my compatriots losing a leg, and bleeding out in an anteroom. A primitive security measure had seen to another; upon gaining entry into the navigation room, a mechanically-discharged spike had punctured his breathing apparatus at neck-height. I turned back after this; there were no signs of life or movement on the entire ship, and the navigation room was the last sealed chamber that had proved opaque to our sensors.

I am not a relic hunter, otherwise I might have proceeded. We are not employed to risk our lives for trinkets, nor do we think trinkets worthy of our cause. So I turned back. A Deliverancer searches for the unsavoury experiments of our wayward forefathers; the biotechnical remnants of an age *long scorned.*

We searched the first ship as a precaution, more than anything. We detected no signals, no signs of life, but an old ship is an old ship, and if certain areas cannot be scanned from the outside, then they must be entered. *Infernal amalgamations of man and machine can not be suffered to live,* or so the tenets of the Bodily Sanctity dictate. Our forefathers caused millennia of chaos with their wanton transhumanism; if something could be spliced into the human genome, then it was done. Sometimes even for little benefit; if science could be advanced in any way, then it was; if it couldn't be considered advancement, then it still proved valuable, to show what could and could not be done. It was a dire fate indeed to end up as one of their null hypotheses. And plenty of people did.

Pure humans, those that had retained bodily autonomy and rejected biomechanical interference, were a scarce minority. A minority that had risen up after the inevitable degeneration of the transhumanists led them to depravity and fiendishness; all traces of their humanity gone, replaced only by mechanical barbarity. It had been a relatively easy conquest for the last true humans, united by unwavering faith in the sanctity and divinity of flesh and blood, to overcome the decrepit biomechanical hordes that then populated the known universe.

All that was left now was cleanup duty; lonesome squadrons of Deliverancers deployed to the Outer Reaches, to little-known star systems, to purge both planets and vessels of the last vestiges of these biotechnical organisms. *They could not be suffered to live.* Not because of any threat of them rising up as we did; but because their wretched existence was an affront to Bodily Sanctity. It was up to us to put them out of their misery. *To provide Deliverance.*

After some effort, the two Deliverancers in front of me managed to get the door open. The primitive circuitry stood little chance of resisting even the most basic of our Illumination Protocols, delivered through the devices embedded in the backs of our suit-gloves. It took no more than a few minutes for the devices to attune to the electronics and the code binding the door in front of us, and then override them.

The grinding and the sparks that ensued let us know that this door had not been activated in a long time. We walked through into the airlock and repeated the process at the next door; again, not much effort.

However, when the next door popped open, we were greeted by a series of strange noises. Electrical buzzing and mechanical clanking accompanied the switching-on of automatic lighting, which illuminated a large mess-room in front of us. These noises were immediately followed by skittering sounds, the unmistakable sound of metal-on-metal.

I frowned and looked around. Nothing was immediately visible, but I disliked what I'd heard.

On the first ship, we'd heard exactly the same thing. We panicked, but there was nothing there. Just the sounds of ancient circuitry screaming, awoken for the first time in millennia, and disturbing the metal and detritus that surrounded it.

The second ship, though, was a different affair altogether.

During that excursion, one of the men with me had fallen moments after we heard similar noises. Spark Sentries. Common biomechanical monstrosities, given life by our forefathers, birthed for the purposes of security and whatever other twisted whims that suited the men of that cursed age. A creature born of spliced DNA of the dog and the bear, grown cruelly upon mechanical limbs and claws, proved a formidable foe.

Two of them had come out of the darkness upon either side of a freshly opened door, much like this one, and torn the Deliverancer in two. One bit his neck, the other bit his thigh, and both pulled hard. The result was messy, but me and the remaining Deliverancer shot his assailants full of electrified bolts and put them down.

I remember looking at the one that remained mostly intact after the fight, its empty eye sockets oddly haunting. The flesh was stretched over metal, so thin as to be almost parchment-like; millennia of sterility and stillness had preserved it to a remarkable degree.

My eyes traveled to the base of its skull. Jagged circuit-boards and hooked clips attached to cables were embedded in its head. Through study of recovered specimens, we had gleaned that the purpose of these was to continually inflame the parts of the brain responsible for anger, pain, hunger, and the predator instinct. This, in combination with a Identify-Friend-Or-Foe signal-generating chip implanted in every crew member, meant that they were the perfect tool to destroy intruders.

I could see where the veins became cables at the limbs; the miraculous yet unholy melding of flesh and machine that our forefathers had managed to achieve. Electrical charge provided by the ambient charging facilities within the ship, hooked up to its near-indefatigable core, meant that the beasts would survive for aeons if left untouched. Water, likewise, was provided through advanced osmosis modules implanted in the walls of the ship, which converted ice molecules from outside into condensed water inside. An arcane process of electrical blood regeneration meant that a dim vestige of actual biological life remained in these Spark Sentries, alongside the machinery.

I shook my head in wonder. These secrets were lost to us now. Would we ever find out how to make marvels like these again? The Deliverancers, acting in accordance with Bodily Sanctity, hoped not. These things were unholy, this much was certain; they were targets for Deliverance. That these things lived a pale shade of life, in constant pain, was of little consequence to our forefathers. And yet, beasts like this were but minor targets. Inconsequential.

What we sought out was the ultimate foulness, the final affront: a human-machine hybrid.

At this point, they were mythical. I suspected that some had been found in the past, but were destroyed without further reports of their location or details of their circumstances. The Deliverancers were a paranoid order, forever seeking to destroy without trace in case of the past repeating itself, in case Bodily Sanctity was again violated and a man kept alive through hideous biomechanical means.

That there were men such as this, ancient men, scattered throughout the Outer Reaches in wrecked ships, dormant research facilities on dead planets, and stasis-pods orbiting at safe distances, was certain. The Outer Reaches were a stupefyingly large space, though, and it was akin to searching for needles in a haystack. Scanners picked up anomalous signals; one in every ten thousand would be worth investigating; one in every ten thousand of those would be a hit.

The second ship showed signs of irregular movement, which was why we'd boarded. The signs stopped entirely after we'd killed the two Spark Sentries, and there were no opaque chambers within the ship, so we'd turned back. The last remaining Deliverancer had met with an unfortunate end on his way back, so I was the only survivor of that excursion, too. Now, on my third, I was wary. I was expecting trouble. Our transhumanist forefathers had been very active in this sector, or, at least, they had not succumbed to the same degree of depraved suicidal tendencies that had befallen the rest. If a ship was found at all, it was abandoned by its owners, or they had disintegrated themselves for some unfathomable reason. Three ships in three months was a rarity indeed.

There was silence. The ambient lighting showed benches, long tables, and eating implements strewn all over. There was plenty of detail to distract the eye, but I heard that same skittering again. Instinct kicked in.

I shouted, "one left, one right!" Like marionettes, my two subordinates pirouetted to face left and right, and the flash of boltguns lit up the attacking Spark Sentries. I walked between them and swept the rest of the room to make sure.

They shouted in unison, "Clear!"

"Good job," I said, "exactly as I said. Weapons down."

I had prepared these two with a brief, telling them what had happened to the man who was torn in two. In this sector, the Spark Sentries liked to camp either side of doors when they detected intruders, and ambush those walking through; these men performed admirably in countering this tactic.

The thing about the latter stages of biotech was that there were uncountable minor edits made to genes and to the technology, to the programming — none of it was standardised. The behaviour of these organisms in the Outer Reaches differed wildly from sector-to-sector, and the chance that one might encounter strange new hybrids was high.

I checked back in with HQ aboard the Sanctifier-class that hovered close by, the one we'd embarked from in the landing pod.

-Can you still read the signal?
-HQ: We can.

Interesting, I thought. This showed promise.

Alongside the regular signs of life, movement, heat, and pulses that our sophisticated scanners detected aboard this ship, it also appeared to be intentionally sending out some kind of irregular signal, a "beeping" across all detectable spectrums that repeated at random intervals. This proved nothing, as we had seen similar effects from corrupted code still running within archaic ship's computers, or broken signals emanating from communications systems with wires gnawed through by bored monstrosities.

But I dared to hope. We pressed on. I dropped way-markers behind me at every door we passed through, every corridor we walked down. This meant that we, or anyone with our IFF, could see exactly where we'd been. This drew some attention from my men, but I assured them that it was to help find our way out after we were done. This was a complex ship, a labyrinth, and we were trusting our usual methods: find the sealed chambers which proved opaque to the sensors. If we open them all, kill everything, and the signals are no longer detected, then we're done. No need to go tomb-raiding and risk death via traps.

They were uneasy, but this was uneasy work. I spurred them on.

We came to a room lit by a fantastical mechanical insect-shaped thing on the ceiling; its tail covered the majority of the long room like a strip-light. It filled the room with a dull green illumination. I could barely tell whether this was simply decorative technology or a bio-technical organism; I suspected the latter when I noted that the arms and legs of the thing were metal tubes affixed to the ceiling, as though melded in via heat. Our sensors picked up the vaguest signs of life which could have been simply ambient heat from the ship's core.

If it did indeed live, what twisted imitation of life had it been living for all these millennia? Did that even count as life? At what point was it mere circuitry, at what point did the spark of life become so tiny as to become inconsequential? Was it better to live like this, as no more than an ambient hum in the great song of life, or to pace in maddened feral hunger forever, like the Spark Sentries?

Regardless, we shot the thing to pieces anyway, plunging ourselves into darkness. We pressed on with our torches lit. By the time we reached the end of the next corridor, the lights had failed, and we pressed on more nervously. A high ambient level of infrared radiation made night-vision filters useless, so we relied heavily on the torches.

We came to a sealed chamber; after unlocking it we advanced cautiously inside. Our feet slid along the floor unpleasantly. This was new to me, and new to my men, each of us groaned through gritted teeth. We were used to weirdness in our line of work, but this was something that none of us had expected to encounter in an abandoned wreck.

The substance underfoot was akin to slime. We wore metal-soled boots upon metal flooring which was covered in this slime — it was almost impossible to walk properly. We shone the torches around in panic, sweeping the room with light, but there were too many obstacles, too many things to hide behind.

The atmosphere in here was different. It was colder, and my sensors detected abnormal amounts of water. Maybe there was a leak in here, maybe something had malfunctioned with the osmosis modules, I thought. It didn't explain the slime, though.

Suddenly, I saw something which made me jump in fright as my torch passed over it. I saw, in the darkness, a skull, with what looked like little skeletal hands clutching its head as though in despair. The slipperiness underfoot caused me to fall, and I shouted and screamed in a manner most unbefitting a Deliverancer of my rank.

The next few moments were a blur of flashes and bolts, squelching noises and the clattering of metal on metal. With some effort, we recovered ourselves, and were somehow all standing upright in the middle of the room. I could see the door to the next chamber up ahead, and I was eager to get through it, but we couldn't leave without investigating this room. If it was the source of our irregular signals, then it was the only reason we'd boarded.

We probed around the room with groping fingers of torchlight until we settled upon our prize: a disgusting slug-like creature, absolutely gigantic, as tall as a Spark Sentry and twice as wide. Embedded in its crest, there was indeed a small skeletal humanoid figure. My heart skipped a beat; but it wasn't what we were looking for.

A preliminary scan showed almost instantaneously that this thing was a mere ape-like creature, abhorrently spliced with a gigantic slug-like thing, for purposes unknown. The main bulk of its body was black, shiny, and glistening with mucous. Its rippling skin undulated unpleasantly as it advanced towards us.

This thing made me sick. The worst I'd seen yet. I resolved to deal with it, slow and unthreatening as it was.

"You," I said, nudging one of my subordinates with the tip of my boltgun, "get forward and deal with it."

The man nervously hobbled forward upon the slimy flooring and lit the thing up with bolts. To my disbelief, the slug-thing's skin was merely an inch-or-two thick covering over a hard metallic chassis, and the mucous was already pooling in the holes left in the skin by the bolts. I watched, in horror, as the black, slithering skin began to knit itself back together, in some places over the top of bolts that were embedded in the metal.

"Urgh," said the other man.
"What the hell is this thing?" asked the man who had shot at it, "why was it made?"

I had been pondering exactly that, and had surmised, "it's obviously some freakish biotechnical organism designed to seek out water. I've seen pure-bio creatures like this on wet planets, albeit a lot smaller. Maybe they needed it to seek out water on the ship, maybe they were concerned about their osmosis modules. Maybe they took it to the surface of planets and used it to find water there."

"Yeah," said the shooter, "but why the ape thing? The skeleton? Look at it, it's half metal and half bone. You can see wires and chips. It had some effort put into it."

"Now that, I don't know," I replied, "maybe it needed more brainpower. Maybe they did it just for some sick game, some twisted affront to Bodily Sanctity. We've seen the like before when they needed just enough brainpower for something to seek, but they didn't want it to have a soul."

"What's that? ARGH!"

The shooter's shouts alarmed me, and I flashed my torchlight towards him. To my horror, tons of smaller slug-things had crawled up his legs and were covering him in slime. There was a hole in the venting below his feet, and untold numbers of them had silently crawled around and up onto him. They were each about the size of a shoe.

My first thought was for my own safety. I looked down: nothing. They were wriggling towards me, though. I made for the exit behind us. The shooter was in some distress, and flailing his arms rapidly. The other man stood uncertainly, not knowing whether to help or run. I ordered him to do the latter.

Silently, and unbeknownst to anyone, I used my secret manual override to cut off the shouting man's suit from his oxygen tank. I couldn't risk the man loosing off bolts in panic, and besides, he would make a worthy sacrifice for me to get away freely. I used the same override to fill his veins with sedatives, deployed from within the sleeves of the suit straight into his veins through miniature needles. He lay there, and began to be slowly enveloped by the black mucous-laden mass. *I hate slugs, and I didn't want even one of those things to get within ten feet of me.*

I rummaged around in my utility belt for a couple of grenades, tossed them into the whole mess, and turned around. I gingerly made my way to the exit, trying my best not to fall over. We closed the next door behind us and set a strong lock with our Illumination Protocols, to keep out the slime. Shortly afterwards, we heard a few short explosions from my grenades.

Thankfully, there was no slime here, that chamber having been thoroughly sealed. Where the vents led, how many of them there were, and just how slimy this ship's innards were, I hoped I'd never find out.

We hadn't eliminated the biotechnical slugs, those foul mockeries of animal life, but they could be dealt with later by a larger team of grunts with specialised weapons brought from the Sanctifier. I wanted to move on. I was confident that the slugs weren't the source of our irregular signal because I could hear it, plain as day, whenever it crossed into the audible spectrum of sound. It was coming from the other end of the corridor.

I walked toward it eagerly, dropping a way-marker as I went. "What happened back there?" the other man asked me.

"He died," I said, matter-of-factly.

"Just looked like he fell over and didn't get back up."

"Yeah," I said, "he slipped in all that mucous."

"I saw that, but then it looked like he just sort of gave up. He was panicking like hell, I saw him about to raise up his gun, I thought things were about to get really hairy, and then he just slumped back," the man said as we walked down the corridor. There was a hint of accusation in his tone. "Looked like he couldn't breathe."

"Yeah, well, maybe his apparatus was punctured when he fell. These old ships are full of jagged corners, wrenched-off wall panels, smashed flooring broken pipes and the like."

"I didn't see it puncture," he said, and stopped.

"What are you suggesting?" I said, rounding on him. I opened the comms line to HQ, just to frighten him into submission. Such defiance had already irked me, and was more than enough to earn him harsh discipline in ordinary circumstances. He wouldn't dare repeat it or take it any further while the official comms line was open.

Or would he? Would he call my bluff?

"Nothing."

That's right, I thought, fat lot of good it would have done you anyway.

We moved on, in silence, until we got to the next door. It opened without much trouble, and what we saw inside made us both gasp.

In front of us, splayed out in a truly horrific fashion, was the twitching body of a man. The man was half-flesh, half-metal, and he was a mess of circuits and wires and bones and veins and desiccated skin. His arms were hung out above his head and placed out to the sides, as though they were the wings of an angel, and his head drooped between them.

Wires hung his hands from the ceiling, wires that directly connected to veins, the metallic threads meshing to the skin in ways that made the mind boggle. I looked, in utter wonder, at the medical and technological marvel that hung in front of me; the sickly colour gradient from dull metal to pale skin was fascinating. How did our forefathers do this? What alloys, what gene sequences, allowed the metal and flesh to meld in such a way, as easily as mixing together two types of paint?

The hybrid was obviously alive, and twitching in a most disturbing fashion. It looked like it was in pain. This was so often the case with biotech, and one of the reasons why it came to be regarded as such an abomination; our forefathers knew that pain, hunger, and distress could be used as powerful motivators. And there are widely-circulated folk-tales that they dialed up the intensity of these sensations for sadistic reasons, and even did it to themselves for masochistic reasons, chasing ever-higher inflammations of the senses to augment their experience of life.

Obviously, the end result was suicide. For a lot of them. For some of them, the end result was this, this monstrosity I beheld before me. It was trying to lift its head up.

My subordinate groaned in disgust. Underneath my visor, hidden from sight, I smiled. *Finally,* I thought, *we've found one.*

Quietly, I gave the signal to HQ.

I looked around the room. The purpose of this place was entirely unknown to me. An entirely unfathomable room full of mysterious implements that would set HQ alight with excitement. It was a small room, and in fact, most of the machinery inside it seemed dedicated to the flayed biomechanical man in the middle of it. That the thing was still alive, and with apparently functioning organs, skin, muscle, and sinew, was yet another marvel — I surmised that the ship's core must have some kind of direct route through all this machinery to the flayed man, acting as a kind of life-support system. That the thing was sending out signals - and had the necessary equipment to do so - led me to believe that this was some kind of communications room. A backup, maybe? An SOS signal? Could our forefathers have been so depraved as to use this for a mere SOS signal, a man, trapped in permanent intense pain, knowing nothing but to signal for help?

Was he calling for help for the ship, or help for himself?

Help for himself was help for the ship, I supposed. The old transhumanists were depraved, but they got results. Still, did it need to be a human?

This was a silly question, I knew. It could have been a mere line of computer code. But that's not how our forefathers did things, if they could avoid it.

Could it not have been some lesser creature, though?

Maybe it was only man, with his unique cravings and his increased capacity for misery and desperation, augmented with technology to increase those sensations, that could have kept manually sending an SOS signal for thousands of years.

"Disgusting," said my subordinate, bringing me out of my reverie.

"Yes " I said. Silently, I used the same overrides that had killed his comrade, to no effect.

"Status report," I rapped.

"Healthy," the man said, "systems functional."

"Have you tampered with your suit?" I snapped. I checked the other overrides — the one on his boltgun was still working. I disabled his weapon silently.

The man turned around to face me. "I found needles in the sleeves, and a stopcap on my oxygen tubes that seemed like a total liability-"

"Making modifications to your equipment is punishable by Inquisition."

"Why would it need those things? You - that's what you did to him in there with the slugs!"

I looked at him pitilessly and raised my gun to his face. "Step aside," I said.

Lightning-fast, he raised his own gun and pulled the trigger. Nothing happened.

"Bastard," he said flatly.

"Step aside," I repeated. He obeyed and took a step toward the door. I loosed a single bolt into his helmet, heard his faceplate smash, and watched him crumple. I had moved him to minimise risk to the biomachinery around us; our true prize. I opened the comms line.

-How fares everything aboard the Sanctifier?

-HQ: All in hand. Other Deliverancers dead. Treasure-hunters dead. Non-compliant crew members and staff dead. How fares everything aboard the wreck?

-Specimen secured. Other Deliverancers dead. Bring men aboard to begin studying specimen.

-HQ: Is the way clear?

-Slight slug problem. Bring explosives. And a flamethrower. A big one.

-HQ: Will a Purifier-class do the job?

-No. Bigger than that.

-HQ: Please confirm. A Purifier-class is an anti-tank incendiary device.

-Confirmed.

At this, I closed the comms line.

I hate slugs.

While I waited, I looked up at the flayed man in front of me. I was curious as to how he sent his signals. I looked up his right hand. I noticed that every time the feeble body twitched, wires and tendons contracted in the wrist area, and his hand made a little waving gesture, different every time. A small field-generator in front of his hand interpreted these signals as different patterns of noise, explaining the random nature of the SOS signals.

Every time it twitched, just on the edge of hearing, there came a little groan and a hiss. The thing must have found it excruciating to twitch so, and yet it continued to twitch, and had twitched for thousands of years.

I placed my finger underneath its chin and delicately lifted up its head. The pain in those eyes I could not possibly begin to describe it. What did it want? Did it want to die? To lead somebody here to end its miserable life? Or had its mind truly disintegrated, and it was akin to a robot now, mindlessly repeating the same gestures? Could this thing have spoken, back when it was in use? Back when the ship was crewed, back when it was mobile? I wonder what it said? Did it beg for death then, all those millennia ago?

I wouldn't get anything out of it now, that was for certain, but I said a few words to it anyway.

"I'm sorry, my friend, but you've got a little more to suffer through yet. We're going to reverse-engineer you, you're going to help us reinstate the Art. Transhumanism will rise again, flesh will meet machine, and the stifling influence of Bodily Sanctity will be broken."

Its eyes looked into mine. It understood nothing, but still it stared, mesmerised. It had not sent a twitch-signal in some minutes.

"Who knows how long it'll take to reverse-engineer you, my friend, who knows how long we'll need to discover how they melded you so successfully to this circuitry. But what's another hundred years to you, eh? What's another thousand?"

*Ramek dislikes this future timeline intensely. Men melded to machines? Torturously? Forever? Better to die with a guark in your hand, flesh from seedling to mummy. Ramek does *ahem* have a necessary mechanical eye and arm, from his injuries. But Ramek controls them! Until God withdraws my lifeforce and this flesh becomes food for whol-wigs and thidgeries.*

the ZONE
Brendan Heard

Hartshorn studied the new speaker carefully. He was sallow, perhaps Mediterranean, and stick-thin. Thavermass greeted the assembly with formal charm as he set down his immaculate leather portfolio case, and briefly adjusted his cashmere collar-tie. His eyes had the savannah glow of a night-lion, the artificial lenses not only curing his blindness, but keeping him constantly connected to a net-stream.

This Thavermass is a pure government creature. Hartshorn thought. Thavermass had a beautiful girl with him, some sort of personal assistant. Curly auburn hair, green eyes, and a form-fitting suit. She appeared to have a pet mink on an invisible molecular leash.

"Gentlemen," Thavermass began. There was a low chuckle about the room at this classical professional opening. "The new laws forbidding women from government feeds allow for this old-fashioned language," he smiled, "it is the first of many new official Spaceforce initiatives regarding special branch or high-security, high-priority briefings. Such as this one."

"And what about her?" Hartshorn nodded towards the girl.

"My personal assistant Miss Eudof does not count as an individual, she is company-raised and an extension of me."

"What are we assembled here for?" Interrupted Bjornstad, an older, somewhat fat and strong-featured man who was Hyperdrive Navigation Team Leader. He wore spectacles connecting him constantly to his own feed. *No doubt some busy work-hive of human and AI hyperdrive calculators planing flight paths across the galaxy,* Hartshorn thought. He knew the type well, they usually annoyed him.

"We are here to discuss this, the black zone... gentlemen." Here Thavermass projected from his folder a hologram of their local galactic quadrant, with all major zones and star systems accounted for and labelled. This filled the room before them, and a small portion of the hologram was then outlined in red.

"I'm sure you've all heard of the zone by now. This is its circumference, according to our latest data. As far as we know, almost everything that passes within this area on our hyper-drive circuit..." here Thavermass took dramatic pause, raising an eyebrow.

"...vanishes."

Hartshorn felt a sinking in the pit of his stomach, knowing instantly why he had been invited. He had no lens implants or feed-spectacles. He had no one to impress. He took a glance to Miss Eudof and she was staring at him unabashedly, her long eyelashes fluttered briefly.

Bjornstad emitted a laugh. "Vanished how? Nothing just vanishes from hyperspace."

"That's false," Hartshorn interrupted, staring intently at Thavermass with a wry smile. "The Raptor escape, ten years ago."

"They were smugglers, criminals — that's a con, they faked it and are in hiding somewhere..."

"No," Hartshorn said.

"How do you know? Who the hell are you anyway-"

"Mr. Hartshorn," Thavermass interjected, "is here precisely for two reasons, Mr. Bjornstad. Firstly because he is the company's finest union-buster and company mercenary. And secondly, because he was onboard The Raptor when she experienced her disappearance."

Bjornstad gave a look of angry confusion. "You are a smuggler?"

"Former smuggler," Hartshorn said, casually smoking his caffeine-stick, examining the long legs of Miss Eudof. "Just like you're a former virgin hacker."

The navigator scowled, angrily removing his feed-glasses from his large and obtuse nose. "I'll have you know I am a senior flight planner and a company mineral-treasurer, and you have just signed your own contract release form, smart-bollocks. I'll have you out before this meeting ends!"

"No you won't, fatty."

The navigator went bright crimson with rage, "How's that, smuggler?"

“Because,” Thavermass interrupted the two men, his voice a calm baritone, “for the reasons I stated a moment ago. Hartshorn is a union-buster, a company tough. Dirty jobs. Also a damn good pilot, and finally and most importantly, he survived something like this before. There is no one else, Mr. Bjornstad, in terms of this mission, who is of greater importance to the company, as well as to freightliners and hyperspacers of all stripes, than Mr. Hartshom. Specifically he is less expendable than yourself, I must say, Mr. Bjornstad, as is the whimsy of necessity and fate. Although I do not wish to denigrate your importance either, as a master-plotter.”

Bjornstad seemed to be muttering to himself, but he had nothing further to say.

“So no one else has returned from this dead space?” Hartshorn asked.

“No one. Not since the disappearances began. They are never to be seen again. With very few exceptions, that exception being you, Hartshorn. Your route went right through the right rim of this area, which we think has slowly expanded in circumference since. Everyone and everything else is gone, no explanation, no evidence of disaster, no communication, no warnings, no remains.”

Hartshorn had heard the rumours, but believed the zone to be a fable. Despite what he had experienced, which he remembered as a kind of bad dream or inexplicable force majeure. Even a delusion on his part. But he had heard the gossip, naval freight and space mariners were every bit as superstitious as their ancient earth-ocean naval predecessors.

Boboard’s Stellar Beard! So I’m not crazy.

“How long has this been happening, chairman Thavermass?” Bjornstad asked sheepishly.

“Three years ago we began to notice the pattern. It started with the Whitestar salvage line. We lost 10 major space-tankers in one month following this particular route. Then it began happening with the Kodiak, the Sirius, and the Oregon lines. Mostly freight was lost, but some travel liners, and a few refugee shipments from the miner wars. When a cruiser laden with expensive military clones went missing they came looking to us for answers, officially. It took a little while to figure out why exactly these ships were not reaching their destination, and while we still don't know, we know something is happening to them when they cross this zone, as that's where we lose communication." Here the specified region on the holomap glowed red once more. "Somewhere in this section. Of course you can cross this region of space unmolested, the disappearances occur only when in hyperspace."

"How do you intend for me to find out what this is?" Hartshorn cut straight to the chase, stepping over all further formality. Thavermass gave him a cold look, strategically raising his dark and immaculately shaped eyebrow once more, saying nothing.

Just what I thought. They want me to go into it.

"How did you do it?" Bjornstad asked him. Hartshorn took his time responding, taking a long draw on his caffeine cigarette.

"How did I survive, how did I return from the anomaly? Well at the time I was in the employ of Captain Wegg."

"Wegg the pirate?"

"That's the one, though he wouldn't have called himself that. The cops were onto us and we hit hyperdrive. We had a mini-fleet of sorts, ten ships, I manned a small outrigger, solo. That's how I survived. I was just barely within the limit of... whatever this is. But I saw something, before dipping back out. No one believed me — ruined my more promising early career as a pilot, to be honest."

"What? What did you see?" Bjornstad's bullying had evaporated, and Hartshorn could see genuine curiosity in his eyes now. *He needed to know.*

"First, everything went dark. You know when you travel hyper you still see stars streaking past. Well they were gone, it was all black."

"Everything? Black? That's not

possible!"

Hartshorn just ignored him, "not only black out there, but my controls all went black. Almost total power loss. Also there was a... noise."

"A WHAT?!" Bjornstad was practically hysterical, jumping out of his legless anti-grav seat.

"Please..." Thavermass had his open palms outstretched.

"I heard a noise, it was eerie, like the sound of a distant large animal, or like heavy metal objects rubbing against one another loudly. Like a droning groan."

"You imagined it! Or it was your outrigger."

"Maybe."

"What else happened?"

"I saw a bright light ahead, in the dark, and little lights all heading towards it — I think they were other ships."

"Could you see into the light? What did it look like? A star?"

"Well, it was the size of a star, but it looked like..."

"Yes?"

"Like a... sphere? Almost even... a head? That's how I remember it, I know it is crazy. They thought I was crazy back then."

Bjornstad froze at this, and became so flustered with disbelief that he brought his arms up over his head, and crashed back down into his seat.

"Then my outrigger careened hard right, power was out, no controls. I think that somehow dropped me out of this black zone. Sheer luck. Because my power came back suddenly, and so did the stars. I just... fell out of it." Miss Eudof gave him a pouty look of sympathy, batting her lashes as she petted the mink.

"We have no option but to believe Mr. Hartshorn's story. He has been queried on it many times by company questioners, and under various induced states. He has no reason to lie. We must face up to the fact that what we may be dealing with here is an alien intelligence. That or a rival company with a technological breakthrough we have missed. Something astounding."

"And now you want me to go back there, maybe to never leave. Like no one else has ever left."

"Yes. You'll be paid handsomely. You can retire after this, if you make it back."

Hartshorn considered for a moment, then smiled. "Okay, fine. I'll go. I'm paid to risk my life. I may be expendable but I can't believe you'd just let an expensive hyperspace-ready ship vanish into thin air."

"Understood Hartshorn. But please, you are obviously a valuable company man, don't belittle your importance to us. But yes, we don't intend to waste any expensive ships. It is useless to us if you fail to return. What we have for you is something new. Something experimental..."

"Experimental?"

"We have developed for you a special vessel, which we have aptly named *The Raptor Phase II*. This has been purpose-fit with a self-perpetuating atomic magnet engine. It is our hope this engine will continue to power, and provide hyperdrive, even after you've entered the... zone."

Here Hartshorn noticed Bjornstad sit up and pay close attention, focusing of course on the technology. "You have an atomic magnet-engine?"

"We do."

Hartshorn had been around, so this was another old wives tale that he was accustomed to. But he never expected to be hearing it stated as reality.

"A perpetual motion machine?"

"Yes, you know what it is. This is the only one of its kind. It works, it has been tested. Regular power failure will not affect it, with human maintenance it is self-generating."

"How does it work?" Bjornstad asked.

"Technically speaking it is not for me to say. But it is the only craft of its kind in the universe."

"So, you want us to fly into a nothingness zone, as an experiment, to hopefully see something that elucidates the whole mystery, and then get back out before it swallows us forever?"

"That is correct. Though we might also, in our heart of hearts, hold out a hope that you might recover all that lost company freight."

"Naturally."

"You'll be paid handsomely, much more than usual."

"I certainly hope so. Where is this one-of-a-kind-ship? When do we go?"

"My dear fellow, we are aboard it, and we go now."

At that the conference room walls dropped, revealing the oval chrome space to be a kind of island, encircled by a drop into blackness, and a wider encircling oval of rowed seating, sparsely populated with important-looking men: company officials, familiar political leaders, and scientists. All were decked in the latest megaboss fashions, elaborate and brightly coloured robes and chrome skull-caps, they all seemed to be either radically obese or skeletally thin. A man in a golden crown of dual antelope heads, shorn of hair with his fat face painted in heavy make-up stood upon a promontory overlooking them.

"Excellent work Thavermass. Well, Hartshorn, Bjornstad, I trust you have no objections?"

He recognised the man: CFO Melmog. Hartshorn nodded in return, saying nothing, the smoke from his caffeine-stick drifting up past his calm, ice-blue eyes. Bjornstad began to sweat profusely, realizing now that he was already on a dangerous mission. Hartshorn watched bemusedly as he squirmed, until his terror at objecting was finally overruled by his terror of vanishing down a cosmic sinkhole. "B-but Eminence Melmog, your grace. Surely I can plot the route from here, why do I need to..."

"Object if you like, Bjornstad," Thavermass interrupted, "but there is a need for real-time navigation and re-navigation, if they have a hope of getting back. There's no AI that can match your humanly parsed electronic brain. If you object too much you will be fired. Possibly worse."

Bjornstad went sullen, and did not speak again. He withdrew an icon of Saint Njord and muttered prayers with it pressed to his lips.

"And you, Thavermass, are you going too?" Hartshorn asked calmly, still staring at his personal secretary.

"Yes." Came an answer from the crowd, and a double of Thavermass stood, dressed in regal robes instead of business attire. Hartshorn looked to the first Thavermass, realization dawning.

The man from the rowed seating spoke: "Yes, that is my double, an artificial. He is the one who has been briefing you..."

"And I am the one who will be joining you." The double finished, smiling wryly. "The original is too important."

"What do we need you for?" Hartshorn asked boldly. A hushed gasp was heard among the small crowd of onlookers. Melmog smiled with a strange glee.

"To ensure company policy and company values are adhered to. And let us not forget Uhg."

CFO Melmog clapped his hands like a child. A portion of the floor before Hartshorn opened, and a large chrome platform raised, with a streamlined seat of great proportion, sitting in which was a genetically enlarged giant, about seven times normal human size. Uhg was strapped to the chair by tubes which ran from his chest and out into a console in the seat.

"What the hell is that?" Bjornstad exclaimed, sounding shrill.

"A line-runner, another innovation, already being used by the larger liners."

"Giants as ship-brains," Hartshorn said coolly, exhaling smoke as though nothing surprised him.

Uhg slowly turned his enormous head towards Hartshorn, gazing with gargantuan passive eyes, as Melmog continued: "Uhg is the brain of the ship. He is your life-line to the magnet-drive. In a way. You have but to tell him your needs, he will be responsible."

"So that's it, eh?" Hartshorn said, noticing now a seat belt built into his seat. The entire chrome island they were on was rising up over the amphitheater.

"That is it, my boy! Good luck to you! Not to worry!" Melmog said as they vanished upwards. Above them there was an aquiline vessel into which their platform slotted.

"Welcome to the *Raptor II*." Thavermass said, as his secretary began recording notes on her wrist-tablet. The mink slipped free and crawled into Hartshorn's lap. Their meeting room slotted into place loudly and pivoted, and was now the ship's bridge. They were within a glass dome and surrounded by the vast twinkling stars of space. Uhg gave a nod of his massive head, and they felt the *Raptor* pushing forward in motion.

"What a view," said Bjornstad, suddenly too dazed by the technology to continue wallowing in his fear. Miss Eudof was visibly shaken, and as Hartshorn handed her back her mink she looped her arm into his, and he felt her shapely hip rubbing up against him.

Uhg gave a kind of low grunt, and they heard the hyperdrive engines warming up with a loud and escalating whine. "How long 'til we get there?" Hartshorn heard Bjornstad asking Uhg.

"One hour." Replied the incredibly low voice of the giant.

"By the way Hartshorn," Thavermass said then, while busying himself with some instrumentation. "Miss Eudof is mine."

They had already progressed to looking fondly into one another's eyes, almost nose to nose, and they didn't stop as Hartshorn replied: "Yours? I thought artificial's could not perform..."

"Coitus? We cannot. Regardless, I have a full range of simulated normal possessive emotions, and I am also your superior. The secretary is mine."

At that the whining engines reached a crescendo pitch,

drowning all else out, and the stars about them began to move at an unnatural speed as they slipped into hyperspace.

"How long before we reach target destination now?" Bjornstad asked Uhg.

"Two months, and one day." Replied the slow and booming voice.

They had been travelling for ten years. The ship was somewhat more worn on its interior, and they had all aged. Hartshorn and Miss Eudof now had two young girls, who spent most of their days playing at the *Raptor's* aft, when they weren't undergoing instruction. Luckily the ship had been outfitted with memory banks full of human history, as they were no longer connected to any networks of any kind.

Hartshorn, already not exactly young when they had started out, was now fifty and quite grey. Still his ice-blue eyes shone with a hard light, perceiving all about him with a calm confidence. Bjornstad had been in and out of breakdowns over the years, but had finally accepted his fate and contented himself with his work.

"I think I will wake Thavermass from cryo-sleep." Hartshorn said. "To see if he will see reason." He reviewed in his mind the events of the last ten years.

After setting out and travelling for about an hour their hyperspace route had intersected with the heart of the zone. As expected they entered some kind of timeslip or new dimension of space. All had gone black outside. Just as Hartshorn remembered.

Only this time they had the atomic magnet engine, and luckily it did indeed work as expected. They had power. But not fully as expected, they were not able to jump into hyperspace. They only had sub-light speed, not as a malfunction of the engines, but as a property of the anomaly they were within.

They all saw the glowing, star-like head that Hartshorn had seen as a smuggler, but at a distance, far enough that it was a bright star to the naked eye. It was the only destination to strive for in the blackness, they had no point of location, no map or compass, and they were easily a million light years in any direction into the heart of the anomaly. Their travelling speed to the object, without lightspeed, was now a matter of many years. But they had no other option, and they had set off.

Along the way they had come across the drifting hulks of many dead ships. Often they boarded them, taking supplies and compiling a record of their stories. Some had completely lost even emergency battery power and seemed to have died and been exposed to space early on. Others had survived for some time, so that they found the crews had died of age or loneliness, drifting slowly forward to the winkling star. When viewed through a telescope Hartshorn was delighted to see it did indeed resemble a great golden head, surrounded by fiery tendrils of long hair. He felt there was a distinctly female quality to it.

They even found Hartshorn's old smuggling crew, with Captain Wegg aboard, now an ancient dried out mummy, still seated at the helm. Hartshorn had saluted him, and withdrew from the captains mouldy pockets a recorder pin he had recalled him using. Hartshorn went through this over the years, and even consulted it from time to time in reflection, as it was the dying recordings of his old captain, and his years drifting in the zone, lost.

One ship they came across had a crew that had gone generational, spawning progeny who knew only life aboard their ship. These too had died from starvation, except for young twins they had rescued in time, a boy and a girl, who now played with Hartshorns own children. The Raptor II was the only ship with any power of propulsion at all in the zone.

"Are you sure you want to wake Thavermass?" Eudof asked in a worried tone, breaking Hartshorn's reminiscence.

"It's time." And with that Hartshorn armed himself with a stun gun, and went to the escape pod which was Thavermass' prison. It didn't take long to defrost the artificial company man, and he was now the only crew member who had not aged. Hartshorn was not certain he would have aged anyway, as an artificial.

"Thavermass, do you recall why I froze you in the escape pod cryo-chamber?"

"I think so."

"Tell me."

"Because after a month into our long trek I flew into a rage over my secretary and tried to kill you."

"That is correct. Now you may still feel emotional about that, as for you that was something that occurred hours ago. For me it has been ten years."

Thavermass shook his head, amazed. "Ten years? I'm sorry, it was so unprofessional of me. I won't do it again."

"I can't trust you Thavermass, but we need you. We'll need you soon. We are getting close now, we can see the star-thing. Whatever's going to happen, it will finally be happening soon. You should be part of it."

"I understand. You all look so old."

"You're no longer the boss, Thavermass."

"My brain has been frozen for so long, let me see the thing now, as we approach it."

Two months passed uneventfully, until they finally drew close to the object, what felt to them like the last object in the cosmos, or the object at the center of creation. As they neared they could see a golden glowing head, it's long hair flowing as if billowed by some energy, like a stream or wind. Each strand of hair was like a flaming snake or river, thrilling with light and energy, like electrified jellyfish tendrils. Its eyes glowed like twin suns, but they sensed great age from the thing. A tiredness in her.

The lost ships they had been sent to rediscover were one by one drifting into the head's open mouth. With each that entered she seemed to grow slightly, and her tired blue-sun eyes would blaze white for a moment, and her hair thrill and wave like tentacles of kelp. As they drew closer, their ship felt a pull now from the object, stronger than gravity, but having still their magnet engine, they were able to hold fast, and sustain an orbit about the thing.

And there they stayed, observing, for another several months. Over time Bjornstad developed a theory that the thing was growing by one tenth its mass with every ship it swallowed. But that at the same time it exhibited attributes of a neutron star, or that of a sun in late stage death.

One day Uhg said, through his giant mouth, now surrounded by long white beard-hair: "We must go into it."

"Uhg has gone crazy, we must deactivate him from the ship." Thavermass said instantly, but Hartshorn said nothing.

He looked to his wife, Eudof, knowing Uhg was right, and said to her: "You must go with the kids, in an escape pod. We will shoot you as far away from here as we can."

"He's right," Bjornstad added in a solemn whisper.

"You've all gone mad. After all this time, you'll destroy the mission!" Thavermass grabbed a nearby prying tool, and stood guarding the main controls.

"Don't do this again Thavermass, you've already been frozen for ten years."

"I am here to protect company interest...."

"Uhg controls the ship, you won't achieve anything guarding those controls."

Thavermass looked desperate, a look Hartshorn had not seen in him until now. *So the artificial has a will to live.*

"You've all gone mad, while I slept, something happened to your brains, this thing has affected them."

"That may be true, Thavermass." Bjornstad said. "But to us, that just means that you missed out on something. We are going into that thing. There's nowhere else to go anyway."

"Look at it! At her! That giant cell out there, that dying feminine sun." Hartshorn said. "We've had ten years of looking and studying, drawing every conclusion you can imagine, waiting for this moment. Do you know what she is, Thavermass?"

"Do I? Are you saying you do?"

"It is an egg. An ovum. Something is waiting to be born. Here, in this nothing-spot. We can all sense this. Destiny brought us to this place, it is beyond human concern now. My only hope is that my children can survive, and have a life, before their time comes. Because ours surely has, Thavermass. This is a thing waiting to be born. Once we enter her, like a seed. Like a sperm, Thavermass, and we impregnate the new universe, it is waiting for us. We will be the genetic imprint of this new cosmos. It is a great privilege. Especially for a lab-made artificial cockroach like you."

"I can't... I can't believe what I'm hearing. This is not the company mission..."

"Why on earth would I ever dream of unfreezing a jerk like you?"

Thavermass' face became dark with umbrage, and with an alarming, almost inhuman rapidity, he launched himself over the console at Hartshorn. He had clubbed the now much older man in the temple, and managed to shove the sharp end of the tool into his side, before Hartshorn grabbed his jaw with one hand, and his hair in the other, and twisted his head all the way around, like an owl, with a loud crack.

Thavermass flopped over onto the ground. While he did bleed blood, it was mixed with a strange clear fluid. Artificial or not, he was dead.

"You are hurt!" Eudof fussed over her wounded husband. "Is it serious?"

"Sure, but that doesn't matter now. You know that. What matters is that you try to make it out, with the little ones."

Uhg and Bjornstad looked away, as the family said their tearful goodbyes, and Hartshorn led Eudof and the four kids to one

of the escape pods.
"If you make it back, if the old universe is still there, try to explain what happened. It's probably not possible, as we can hardly explain to ourselves. Look for me in the new stars, I will be there."

They tearfully kissed goodbye, and soon after the pod was shot out, with as much force as the magnet engine could provide, and when it had gone beyond the range of their sensors, the mortally wounded Hartshorn gave the order, and Uhg steered the *Raptor* into the mouth of the golden head. Inside it was so bright they could barely see. The walls of the head were translucent but electrified with light swells and rivers of energy. At the center was an oval, also somewhat translucent and glowing, with pinprick vessels all impacted and stuck upon its surface.

"Do we have laser energy, Uhg?"

"Just enough."

At that they cut a slice in the oval's energy-flesh, and being the only ship with power, they navigated into the egg.
From their escape craft Eudof and her children soon saw a brilliant flash, that turned everything white about them. Then, gradually, as they travelled, they began to see stars again.

A strange story, no? It is to suggest the universe is not at all what it seems, and is bounded by laws even more bizarre than those already speculated? As though it were itself, and time with it, a kind of biological mechanism — a living being? Which dies and is replaced by progeny? But how can that be? And where is the outer boundary of that being? Or its parents?

Ramek's brain hurts.

The Gnomish Deepwood Gneeds
YOU
To read Toadstool!
www.toadstoolmag.com

The Psychic Assassin

By Jason lupus
& Brendan Heard

The colonization of Mars ended in a somehow unexpected yet typically human fashion. A power struggle. Thus began a long period of warring states, with the petty squabbles of bio-dome clan lords bringing rival plexi-glass kingdoms to the blood-ridden planet. During the age when the polar caps were nuked with bombs of a magnitude never-before seen, and the many-generations-long process of creating an atmosphere begun, great feudal lords rose...

Marcus entered the domed city surrounded by the men of his lord, Ironlung. He was covered in red dust from the thunderous desert storm outside, and he brushed this off as he marched into the red-stone halls of Castle Ironlung. He had just crossed the treacherous wasteland pits and canyons — beneath swirling, sinister skies, which toiled desperately to create a nuclear-winter atmosphere above their heads.

He entered his kingdom dome via his master's private entrance, which he was permitted to use as a close loyal servant. It was a guarded cave in solid rock, which adjoined a long plexi-glass tube running underground directly into the castle walls.

He reached his private apartment in the old fortress. The walls were crude stone blocks, but it was clean, with expensive glass furniture, and green with plants of many varieties, Martian and Terran. Once inside he removed the wrathful mask of the deity Angmak, which provided oxygen when walking outside the dome, and removed the associated tubes and backpack. Once alone in his inner chambers, he gave prayers and offerings to his ancestors, and the genii loci of Mars before the sacrificial altar of his private chamber. Retiring to sit in a lotus Zen position, Marcus meditated upon his soul and his physical mortality. His sabre-sword and fire-pistol lay at rest beside him as he sought for his balancing inner peace, as was his practice every day upon returning from his vigil.

Ironlung's private bodyguards arrived at the door, requesting an immediate audience. Marcus had been expecting this, and soon, flanked by massive guards, a dark figure dressed in thick black velvet robes entered, his face hidden behind a hood. Marcus was one of the few confidants Ironlung would visit personally,

"My friend," Ironlung said, and Marcus could just make out grinning teeth beneath the hood. Marcus bowed low, understanding it was a great honour to be referred to in such a familiar way: "The enemy is dead, lord."

"Good news, Marcus, were you detected?"

"I am never detected, the enemy has gone peacefully in his dreams, none of his people had any awareness of psychic assassination."

"You have done well, but I need one more favour from you, if you think your powers are up to it?"

"My powers are ever-ready."

"Our northern enemies, the Tiger clan, want to exploit resources that are rightfully ours. They have already tried to subvert our temples for their political ends, with their new and supposedly peaceful emissaries preaching their foreign philosophy. Their leader shall be the next target of your dream-attack."

"He shall be killed, lord, without a drop of blood."

Ironlung said nothing further, and with his men he went to leave, as Marcus lay prostrate and prayed to the shrine of Sekhor and Akmat, acknowledging their protection as he focused his mind.

"A religiously pious warrior," Ironlung said to his men, admiring his remonstrations as they departed.

After some time Marcus pressed a hidden wall button and revealed a secret oval chamber, just large enough for himself. After removing his clothes he entered this and sat cross-legged, and the red stone wall closed up again behind him. This was his stop-box, where he prepared his mind, studied his tantras, and focused his psychic weaponry. He required absolute privacy, hidden away from his enemies and even his allies.

He meditated once more upon his death and recited the sacred scriptures for the protection of heaven and the deities. His body was covered in talismanic tattoos - dragons and sacred scriptures, to protect his psyche from evil and negative spirits. As his meditation began Marcus felt a sudden intrusive mind in his thoughts, a spirit medium from a local temple was there, as he often was, channeling a mantra of success in the wars. The mantra went: "Once our leader's enemy is dead, conflict shall cease for years to come."

He acknowledged and then easily blocked the medium from his private thoughts. Marcus showed kindness to mental-vendors and mantra-priests, knowing he would benefit from positive Karma for doing so. In his mind the spirit medium projected a final visual, wearing the mask of his temple deity: he bowed his head in thanks.

Marcus noted then with curiosity that the priest had never projected a visual before.

He thought of this at first as a matter of casual observation, and then with a sudden reaction of violence. He had a split second to counter and protect himself from a sudden psychic attack. He blocked it with a mental wall, though he felt a kind of pain, like his mind had been faintly injured.

I have never been attacked myself, while at home, not in this way. Nobody until now has known who I was. They would have to know his location, know about his wall-pod. He rose and left the secret room, knowing the enemy had to be close, probably in the building, but stopped himself from grabbing his fire-pistol and heading back to the door. *No, a better plan is to feint him back in.*

He decided to take a break, to goad the enemy, whoever they were, into following him around. *They would slip up, and he would get a look at them, or a sense of them.*

Marcus left the castle on his hoverbike and parked it at the entrance to the underground necropolis. He genuflected respectfully before entering, and once down inside among the tombs of his ancestors, he gave more prayer. He did not risk retreating fully into his mind. But he caught a sense of the mental intruder once more, still in the guise of the innocent mantra-vendor

He must be near to still be broadcasting, he must have followed me.

Marcus walked the catacombs, then retraced his steps, stopping intermittently, checking every nook and cranny both physically and with his mind. There were others who were here to pray, he had no way of telling which of them might be the assassin, as the killer would have a foolproof false mental front. But Marcus detected no one following him.

He did at one point notice a druidess, heavily robed, who appeared inappropriately buxom, and seeming to wear beneath her holy robes a leather jumpsuit, also strange and unsuitable. But she was busy at her prayers before the death mask of Marcus' ancestor Somak.

I detect absolutely nothing from her. Also a female psychic assassin? He had never yet heard of one. But a wise man was ready for a first-time occurrence.

After studying her at her prayers, and penetrating her thoughts and finding only prayer-focus, he passed through the various crypts, and emerged in a park, with trees so high they brushed the top of the dome.

I am useless, I am dead, if I cannot detect the source of the attack. But I have my last hidden weapon, of which no one knows anything. He had blocked even from himself the knowledge of this weapon, with only a reminding memory remaining. *That it exists,* and that it could be called upon only when totally exposed and traversing the psychic plain. Mounting his hoverbike he took another special-access route back to the castle of Ironlung.

Back in his chambers, he went to his bed and sat cross-legged upon it. Whoever the assassin was they knew the location of his secret chamber, his stop-box, so it was no longer of any use. Whoever it was would monitor him now until he fell asleep, or fell prey to some other distraction. There was nothing for it but to meet the assassin head-on, and hope to surprise them both with his secret weapon.

Whatever that was.

He was determined to create the illusion he was performing a regular routine, pretending that he believed himself safe. He performed a typical pre-sleep ritual, and laying down this time, slipped into his mind. He acknowledged normally the friendly signal from the mantra-vendor, awaiting the inevitable attack. But nothing happened, it was not the assassin in disguise this time, it was the actual priest.

He scoured the pre-dream mindscape. He saw in his imagination a recreation of the harsh Martian sandstorm, which he then walked through. In this vision he was naked, and without mask, as only can be done in imagination. In the distant mountain he saw the death mask of Somak from the crypt, but carved from the solid rock at monumental proportion.

White stone, the brows of Somak furrowed.

He had a sense. *Who was here with him?* There was no indication of anyone yet, yet there was a feeling that he was being observed. A mythical Kytan bird flew high overhead, like a great dragon, oblivious as Marcus was to the cutting storm. As he walked the sand beneath his feet suddenly became loose. He stopped this notion in his thoughts, yet in the daydream the sand only became looser, until he was sinking.

So, it begins, he thought.

Imagining himself levitating he freed himself from the sinkhole. Beneath him it opened to a great swirling gyre of sand, a rapid and mesmerizing vortex, spinning away to nowhere. In the dark at the heart of the gyre he saw a single giant eye open and stare at him. A beautiful blue and long-lashed eye, a female eye.

He allowed himself to stare at this for some time, as his dreamscape body grew larger, and the eye blinked coquettishly, as Marcus grew to outsize the entire face of Mars, until he could cup the entire planet in his palm, and this he did, holding and crushing it, until nothing but little rivulets of sand remained, streaming from his fist as from an hourglass. The gesture was superficial, he knew he had not contained the enemy so easily. Contained *her*.

He had a vision then, his mind recreating the catacombs. The druidess he had been studying, he recreated that memory in his mind. Every inch of the crypt wall and floor, the scurrying wall-spiders, the face of Somak, the woman's leather under-attire. In this new memory he walked over to her, trying to see her face. He reached out and pulled back her hood. Beneath it her leather undersuit covered her head, exposing only her face, which did not turn to him, and as he reached out to grab her chin and turn it towards him, she turned into snakes, which fell as a bundle to the stone floor and writhed everywhere. He lost control of his imagination once more, and before he could counter-think a large snake had begun swallowing his foot, then his leg, quite rapidly. The snake had long eyelashes around blue eyes. Now it swallowed him completely, and he was suffocating in its innards.

He thought of himself as a human inferno, alight all over with nuclear flame. But she somehow suppressed this thought, and his flame winked out. He caught her by surprise by imagining himself miniscule, first as a germ, then an atom, slipping through a stream of atoms to reform in another dreamscape.

He was on the face of Mars again. Inconspicuously, except that he was colossal in size, and naked, save for his mask of Angmak. He dreamed that he didn't need to walk, but floated just over the sand. He dreamed there were incredible gold pyramids at the distance, like mountains on the horizon, and the sky was bright azure, like those of Earth, and there was atmosphere and breathable air. He scoured the red sand and rock for her, in every direction, not touching anything, not allowing any stray thoughts. The bright sunlight shone off his mask as he turned this way and that.

He could see stars twinkling through the blue above him, Earth itself shining brightly. Then the pure azure cracked, and the sky broke like it was the Ironlung plexi-dome, and great shards of blue fell about him. One lanced his shoulder, and he felt the sharp pain, as real as anything. *She has struck a blow!*

The space beyond the now shattered sky was a nightmare, both black and sucking and red and violent. He could hear female laughter echoing off the hills and pyramids at the horizon, all about him.

He looked to his split shoulder, red with crimson gore, the pain excruciatingly real. He tried to focus on imagining it healed, but too late, her wound was all-encompassing, he could not see past the pain. As he looked upon it, the wound seemed to grow, so that his flesh was peeling off, revealing the rough bone beneath. He cried out in agony as he began to transform into death. He could not save himself.

Now! The secret! Now! Strike, with whatever it is! The secret weapon!

All other thoughts were suddenly side-stepped out of — they were shrunk and compartmentalized and analyzed unemotionally. He was outside himself, and casually watched the naked colossus of his own body become a skeleton. Then he saw her. He saw her black leather jumpsuit, saw her hiding behind some Martian rock, watching. He no longer had a body, and he made a wind of his spirit and bore down upon her, entering her mind, directly into her thoughts. She was utterly undone.

He saw everything about her instantly, and in that same instant he killed her. Believing herself dead — she was.

Marcus awoke with a start, out of the dreamscape and back in his room. His daydream had evolved into a sleep-dream, but even as she had plotted to kill him psychically, her physical self had been ready to make double-sure the job was finished.

Her beautiful leather-clad body dropped from the ceiling as he opened his eyes, a curved dagger in her hand. But having just killed her in the dream, her body fell to the bed now lifeless, and he pushed her corpse off of him, the knife clattering away on the cold stone floor.

She was good. She was very, very good.

He was still reeling from a two-fold realization from the vision.

Firstly, his secret weapon had been nothing at all. It had been nothing more than the belief that there *was* a secret weapon. His confidence in its supposed mastery had allowed him at the crucial moment to step outside himself, by some hidden agency of faith. He felt no pain or remaining injury from her attack at all.

The other revelation was bitter, and he felt a storm of anger within him, overriding all other thoughts. Taking up his fire-pistol and holstering it, he left his apartments. Outside there were guards stationed, and Marcus looked at them coldly, examining their reaction. *Were they surprised to see him?* They showed no reaction. He walked unhindered to one of the castle public balconies in the great eastern turret.

Here he looked out over his city. The city of Ironlung.

Then he looked up to the great dome, seeing the night sky beyond it: the twinkling stars, reminding him of his psychic battle, and the sky that had shattered. For in the instant that he had entered her mind, he saw the full truth. It was not the enemy who had hired her to assassinate him. Ironlung himself had hired her, after acknowledging her superior abilities, and knowing that Marcus knew too much to be casually retired, he had been deemed expendable.

Expendable. Looking up at the dome protecting the city, he thought hard as he stared at it, and then he thought harder, projecting all his psychic might.

Slowly a crack began to form in the thick plexi-glass sky.

It would seem, scruntlings, that poor Marcus had simply had enough? But wouldn't you? Betrayed by your feudal overlord for a sexy psychic assassin?

Ramek, too, would let them all die.

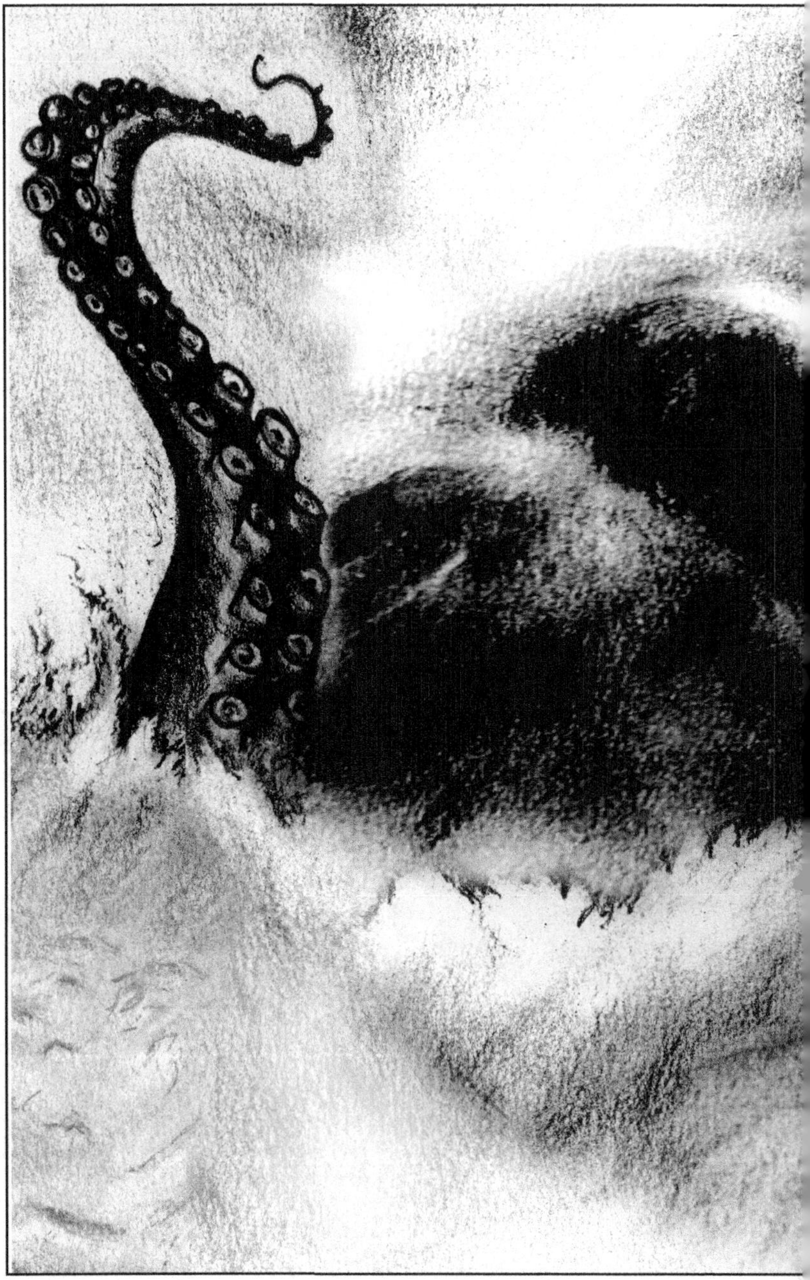

KING'S BLOOD

By Mark Straker

697AD. Cutting through the sea not far off the south east coast of Britannia, a band of Saxon warriors journey in search of their fortunes.

At least that was the case for most. For Hrothgar, it was a search for the battle, the glory, and the reputation. Hrothgar was in it for immortality. He had more to live up to than most, for it was said Hrothgar was a descendant of Horsa himself.

To look at him you would certainly believe it, for he was built strong and stood far above most men of his day. He wore his long and dark-blonde hair in a mullet, tied back, with a short beard and long thick mustache. His face had a noble appearance, but his piercing, pale blue eyes gave him a serious and intimidating look. His brown fur cloak covered his thick leather and mail armour, protecting it from the salt sea sprays. His helmet, buckles and jewelry were all finely decorated and the envy of every man on the boat, particularly his sword, which was finished with a silver raven head-pommel. All had been passed down from his grandfathers after living a life of conquest.

Hrothgar was born in the Kingdom of Essex to a noble family, but had traveled to the northern shores of the continent to the land of his forebears, recruiting kin and companions to aid him on his adventures. He was confident in the ability and quality of each man, and knew they had a hard road of fighting ahead. They were to land in the Saxon port town of Gipeswic (Ipswich) and travel to Weleas, where they would aid their Saxon brothers in the fight against the Celtic kingdoms there.

While pondering these things Hrothgar was brought back to his senses by a freezing spray of sea water and a call from Osric.

"My lord!" He exclaimed, while pointing out to the waves.

Hrothgar quickly stood and scoured the area. He saw a small upturned boat, with what looked to be someone struggling to hold on.

"There!" Hrothgar pointed and

yelled over his shoulder to Aculf, who was on the rudder. They drew closer and saw it was a woman. "Bring us up along side her!"

The men stopped rowing and slowed the boat. Hrothgar leaned over the side and hooked her in as they passed.

Coughing and spluttering sea water, she collected herself on the deck, and slowly sat up. "Thank the Gods for you lads. I was collecting my crab traps at sunrise for a day's trading at Gipeswic, when wind and tide took me out. I could not get back no matter how hard I tried." She stood, wringing out her soaked blonde hair and tattered blue dress.

"Well find a seat." Hrothgar told her. "Fortune favours you, for Gipeswic is our destination also." He could see the coast of East Anglia on the horizon, under a blanket of intimidating storm clouds.

Turning to face the men he said: "Brothers! There aren't many hours of daylight left, so let's have at it". The men gave a "Heave!" in unison.

They had not managed to get much further before the weather turned, and dark storm clouds came upon them with unnatural haste. The heavy rain, high winds and encroaching thunder began to push them back out to sea.

"Row men!" Hrothgar shouted as he assumed a seat to lend a hand on the oars. "Row for your lives! Do you want to be out here all night?!" Lightning flashed and lit up his face as he roared.

For some time they toiled against the elements, trying to reach the shore. Looking around him he saw the woman they had rescued wedged between the baggage, making hand gestures like she was praying. He saw struggle and exhaustion on the faces of his men. Finally, looking at Osric and getting a shake of the head, he shouted out. "That's enough men! Get the oars in and hold on!"

The sun had set. Their fate was now in the hands of the Gods. The storm carried their small vessel out to the cold northern seas, on colossal black waves.

For hours they were tossed around under thundering skies, wondering if they would ever see the light of day again. Rain lashed their faces, men threw buckets of water over the side as fast as they were able, hoping the ship wouldn't sink. Aculf did his best on the rudder to avoid taking the waves side on, only getting glimpses of them in the flashes of lightning, which were numerous. It was then that Aculf sighted something. In the sparks of light he saw a silhouette... a rocky peak in the distance.

Land.

"Lord Hrothgar! There! Look! There!" Aculf yelled as loud as he could. Hrothgar looked and saw, rising to his feet feeling a sense of relief.

"Right men! You see it? You want to live? Get on the oars and get us there!" Hrothgar cried out over the thundering noise of the storm. The men took up their positions and began their labour. Hrothgar looked down at the woman who was still huddled away. She gave a slight nod of encouragement and smiled. Strangely, she seemed the most calm and collected person among them.

Suddenly and without warning, a hard thud came from under the boat.

"Rocks Aculf! Mind the Rocks!" Hrothgar shouted to the rear.

"None have been sighted lord!" Aculf replied.

They were interrupted by the loudest, deepest, bellowing noise they had ever heard, to which they covered their ears, their legs shaking with vibrations. This was followed by another thud against the bottom of the boat, this time lifting it slightly out of the water.

Hrothgar and Osric looked at each other as the boat crashed back down. It was then, in the flicker of lightning, that they saw it. A huge tentacle-like arm towering over the aft. Then another. Not unlike that of an octopus or squid, but far larger and with long streaks that pulsed with a turquoise glowing light. It was like something not of this earth. Before anyone could shout words of warning or get to their weapons, one of the tentacles slammed down in the center of the boat, splitting it in two, crushing men and throwing others into the air. Chaos and confusion ensued, as the sea below them glowed with the blue-green pulsing of the Behemoth below them. Glowing tentacles coming for different men could be seen in the eerie gloom. The razor sharp teeth of the suckers embracing each victim tightly, as they were dragged to their graves in the icy depths.

Hrothgar, Osric, the woman, and a few others managed to reach what was left of the front of the boat, clinging to it while fighting to stay above the freezing water. Hrothgar searched around him for the rest of their broken vessel, only to catch a glimpse of it being smashed to pieces and his men crushed by the Behemoth.

"No!" Hrothgar roared, feeling a rush of anguish for his men. He looked back in the direction the land had been spotted and saw that it was not far. He was now trying desperately to shout over the storm and the roars of the creature, which was still busy picking off the men who remained floundering in the water. "Kick everyone! Toward the land! It's our only chance, kick for your lives!"

Luck was with them, finally, and the waves were helping wash them toward the shore, which they approached rapidly. But as they went the waves swelled and broke over the Behemoth's head as it pursued them. Its eyes rising just above the waterline, pulsing with an alien neon turquoise intensity.

As they rode what they hoped would be the final wave into shore, the Behemoth exposed its huge spike filled mouth, letting out a rumbling growl, lunging at them with its tentacles. But the wave finally crashed onto the shore and spilled the survivors out onto the rocky beach. The Behemoth smashed into the steep underwater slope of the shore, the water now too shallow to support its hulking mass, it thrashed around just off the shoreline in chaotic anger. Hrothgar sat up, coughing, in a daze. He looked upon the Behemoth, pulsing its crazy colour, as it eventually surrendered and shoved its queer bulk back out to sea, submerging once more to the depths. Hrothgar let out a sigh of relief and exhaustion as he collapsed onto the wet sand.

After having a moment to catch his breath, he heard the voices, laments and confusion of the remaining survivors around him. Shouts of disbelief, anger, and grief. He knew he had to try and regain control of the situation before he faced a mutiny.

He stood up, looking around. The storm was starting to ease and the moon's light was beginning to break through the clouds, providing a small but vital bit of visibility on their surroundings. Osric came stumbling over, steadying himself on Hrothgar's shoulder.

"My lord! Thank the Gods!" He puffed and panted in relief. Hrothgar was relieved to see him too, Osric was one of his oldest and dearest friends, one he knew he could trust completely. Looking along the shore, Hrothgar could see what looked to be the remains of a jetty and ruined stone harbour building. They gathered what survivors they could and made their way to this. Hrothgar did his best to seem unaffected by the extreme bad luck of events, for the sake of his men.

Upon examining the building he discovered it was empty, but he was grateful to find some remnants of a thatched roof which they could shelter under. He cleared space on the floor and searched for any kind of boat that may have been left down on the jetty. Finding none, he returned to the ruin where Aculf was helping survivors inside. He patted Aculf on the back and looked in the doorway. Only a handful seemed to have made it, filling him with a deep sadness.

"How in the name of Tiw's arse did you survive at the back of that boat?" He turned asking Aculf.

"When that thing struck the boat in two, I got catapulted through air to toward the front, then I hung onto what was left, just as you did."

The two of them could not help but share a quiet laugh together, thinking of Aculf flying through the air.

"The Gods must have a sense of humour." Hrothgar replied. "Now get yourself in there and rest up, we'll work out our next move at first light." He heard footsteps coming up the rocky beach behind him. He turned to see a shape, carrying something unseen, emerging from the dark. It was Grimbold, one of the recruits from Germania, carrying the woman they had rescued, unconscious.

"She's alive, beyond that, I don't know." Grimbold said.

"I'll take her." Osric asserted as he emerged from the ruin. He took the woman and carried her back inside.

"What was that thing?" Grimbold asked.

"I wish I knew brother." Hrothgar replied. "I thought such things only existed in myth. It was not of this earth. Go inside and get some rest."

"It was from Gehenna?"

"From somewhere..." Hrothgar said, looking up to the starry night.

Grimbold shook his head.

"I won't be able to rest after that lord. You go. I'll keep watch out here until first light, who knows what else is out here, after that." With this he sat on the stone wall outside the door, Hrothgar nodded and patted his shoulder in gratitude. He went inside and passed out in a heap, next to the huddled mass of what remained of his men.

The rising sun's rays gleamed through the gaps in the stonework of the ruin, awakening Hrothgar before any of the others. He immediately sat up, recalling the events of the night before. He could see the strange glowing colour of the sea-thing in his mind.

It looked to be a fine, calm morning. He rubbed the face and went outside, passing Grimbold still sitting on the wall with his back to him. As he looked out to sea, he asked of Grimbold. "All's well brother?" To no reply.. He asked again, "Brother?"

For a moment Hrothgar thought his heart had stopped,

so shocked he was at what he saw. He slowly started to circle around to face Grimbold, looking him up and down, trying to fathom what he was seeing. It was him alright, but made of stone, stone that looked like it had been there for years, even starting to grow moss.

"Brothers!" Hrothgar shouted towards the ruin. "Awake all of you!" He ran over to Grimbold, still partly in disbelief at what he saw.

To his dismay, *their eyes met.*

Hrothgar realised not all of Grimbold had petrified. His eyes were as aware as ever and filled with purest terror. Muffled screams of panic could just be discerned through the stone which his mouth was now made of. The men and the woman, gathered around this ghastly sight.

"We have to break him free of this!" Shouted Osric.

"Wait! How do we know we won't kill him in the process?" Hrothgar said. Desperately searching his thoughts for a possible reason or cause.

Mantican spoke up. "This is dark magic. Unnatural. We have been cursed."

They all knew Mantican well enough to expect him to say such a thing. He was the strangest and quietest of the troop, but pious. He could always be seen praying and sacrificing to the Gods when he could. They all turned to look at him, desperately wanting to dismiss his claims, but how could they argue otherwise?

"Listen to your friend there!" A voice cried out.

They all hastily pulled their weapons and looked around in all directions. Grimbold's screams had stopped, he was able to hear what was happening around him.

"Up here!" The voice chuckled cheerfully.

It was a quiet and quite high pitched voice, it sounded far away, yet so near. Aculf was the first to see, as he looked up into the dilapidated thatch of the ruin's roof.

A man. A small man, tiny in

fact, no bigger than Aculf's thumb.

He stood smoking a pipe and feeding what looked to be an over-sized and brightly-coloured hornet with a crude looking saddle upon its back.

"*By the Gods...*" Aculf said softy, staring at the man in wonderment.

They all looked at this in amazement, all except for Mortican, who started laughing at the tiny man.

"What's going on here? How is this possible?" Hrothgar finally asked of the man, with an assertive puzzlement.

"Laughing boy over there, he told you." The hornet man replied while pointing at Mortican with his pipe, who was now doubled over in fits of laughter and doing all he could to stay on his feet. "Sorcery, of the foulest and most powerful kind."

Mortican's laughter was now making it hard for the man to be heard, and Hrothgar stormed over and grabbed him by the shoulders. "Pull yourself together you numbskull! Have you lost your wits!?"

Mortican shoved him off, stumbling away down the beach toward the sea, still laughing uncontrollably. Hrothgar returned to the little man and his hornet.

"What is this sorcery you speak of? Who is responsible and where are they? Speak!"

The man scoffed at this as he took another toke on his pipe. "The Warlock in the mountain." He replied. "He's the master of this island."

"An island?! We're on an island?" Osric asked

"Aye." The man continued. "Couldn't tell you where or what it's called mind you. I'm just a merchant who washed up after a storm. Least I was, 'til he did this to me."

"The Warlock did this to you?" Aculf asked.

"Course he did!" The man snapped. "How'd you think I got like this? Summit I ate?!"

He toked on his pipe.

"We need to find a boat to escape, build one if we have to!" Aculf said.

"Sorry to say it, but you're stuck here folks, the monster of the deep won't let you leave." The hornet man explained. "I'd put your friend out his misery too. Spending eternity as a statue sitting there doesn't sound very appealing to me. If you're lucky the Warlock won't kill you too, just turn you into something for his own personal amusement... like me!" Gripping his pipe in his teeth, he climbed up onto his hornet, taking a pair of reigns in his hands.

"Where is this Warlock?! Can we reverse his magic such as this here?!" Hrothgar asked before the man could take off.

"Not that I know of, your friend's stuck like that. The Warlock has a science, a craft he learned traversing the stars. That's where he and that sea-creature come from, some place beyond even Neorxnawang. He went out there astrally, and returned on ships of iron. Not even iron! But strange metals never before seen here. He and that beast, and other things too! But for now he lives on the peak at the other end of the island, you'll find the Warlock there. Not that it will do you any good." He replied, while maneuvering his hornet with the reigns. The insect took flight and with a jockey's exclamation the little man flew out of sight.

Mortican was ranting to himself on the beach, pacing back and forth. Hrothgar rubbed his brow in stress and confusion, as the rest began arguing among themselves about what to do with Grimbold. Hrothgar, filtering through the noise, noticed he could no longer hear Grimbold's cries. Looking at him, he could see his eyes no longer showed the horror and panic as they did before, but were sad, looking at the ground calmly, not moving. Grimbold had heard the little man and knew what had to be done.

"Quiet!" Hrothgar shouted over the group. Even Mortican stopped rambling and paid attention.

"What do you want us to do

here brother?" Hrothgar softy asked of Grimbold, going in close to him. "We will try our damnedest to free you if you wish, but you heard that sprite. I fear it would be a slow and torturous death. Starvation I expect. If you want me to end this nightmare for you, I shall."

Grimbold gave an affirming grunt from behind his stone lips.

"But... but you can't just..." The woman pleaded uselessly.

"Are you sure brother?" Hrothgar asked putting his hand on his stone shoulder. "Are you sure you want to end it here?" Grimbold grunted in agreement once more. The group emotionally said their goodbyes to Grimbold, all except Mortican, who was now on his knees at the shoreline with his head in his hands.

Hrothgar did not have the weapon he would have preferred for such a task, but he had his strength, strength like no other. He moved behind Grimbold and took up one of the large stone blocks which had been used to construct the ruin.

"We will avenge you brother, have no doubt of that." Hrothgar said, raising the block up high. "I'm sorry I led you down this path. Go now to the green meadows and know no more toil, worry, or strife."

Hrothgar brought the block down on the back of Grimbold's head with a powerful strike. Smashing the top half of him to pieces, so that there was nothing left but his legs, still sitting on the wall. They could see from the blood and guts which spilled out of him that their fears were indeed correct. There was only so much of Grimbold which had petrified, the rest completely untouched. It would have been impossible to free him alive.

Hrothgar looked at the sad faces of the group, the woman with her back turned and hand over her mouth who could not watch. He looked toward Mortican, who was now back on his feet. His eyes staring at Hrothgar with an intense anger from under his dark green hood, his throwing axe and dagger were now in his hands.

"You!" Mortican shouted at the top of his lungs pointing his dagger at Hrothgar. "This is your doing! There is no Warlock or dark magic! We are dead! We died on the seas in that storm and have been cursed to wander this place. Thanks to you!" He started laughing maniacally once again. "Son of Horsa my arse!"

Hrothgar interrupted. "Careful brother. I do not wish to kill two of my men on the same day. You are not yourself. If you cannot regain your senses you are a danger to us all, especially in this place."

Mortican continued, laughing. "Such a wretch cannot be descended from such a great man! Pig spawn all of you! I must have been mad in the first place to come on this voyage! We're done for!"

He screamed then at Hrothgar, charging up the beach, consumed by madness and rage.

Mortican flung his throwing axe, which Hrothgar calmly side stepped with ease. Mortican tried desperately to land a blow with his dagger, failing every attempt.

"I'm sorry brother." Hrothgar said.

He diverted Mortican's final dagger-swing down into his chest. Holding it there, Hrothgar forced him to the ground and stared into his eyes as he died.

Getting up and looking back at the group Hrothgar spoke. "I am sorry my friends. Some of what he said is true. You are here because of the path I chose. But we are not dead. Far from it. Here we face the most trying tasks and enemies any of us will every face. And is that not what we live for, as soldiers of Wodan!?" Raising his fist at this, the others looked at each other and nodded. "Now let's not let the trials we have endured thus far defeat us. Come with me to meet this Warlock in the mountain, we will kill this star-traveller, this dog from Gehenna, for all our brothers who have died at the hands of his devilry!"

"You heard him men!" Osric exclaimed with a single clap. "Lets have at it".

Hrothgar's band was now reduced to him, the woman, Osric and Aculf. As well as two other recruits from Germania, Wistan and Framric. They said their words, buried the remains of their friends on the pebbled beach and set about their task.

Now that it was light, they could see the remains of the front of the boat and some baggage which had washed up on shore. They salvaged a few light weapons and what food they could, which they enjoyed immensely. To his relief Hrothgar's sword was still strapped to the bags that he had wedged it between at the front of the boat. His helmet sadly was gone, lost to the deep, along with his cloak.

"What is your name?" Hrothgar asked of the woman they had rescued.

"Devona..." She replied.

"Well, as you can see Devona, we're stranded in a dangerous place here. So best stay close to me, eh? Don't wander and if we get into trouble, do as I say, understand?"

She nodded with a nervous look.

He strapped on his sword and they set out on the path of revenge.

END OF PART 1

Ramek enjoys such forthright tales of chivalry and heroism and violence. Somewhat historical even.

It may even be that you livestock-age humans may learn a thing or two, and begin to see the technological enclosures which surround you. Or perhaps you will just spend a fleeting moment entertained then return to slavery.

The Dream God:

Eternal Life

By Brendan Heard

The Seven Guild Masters had arrived at the sky-citadel atop the Mazda Plain — a flying island of rock which drifted in the atmosphere over the blighted world of Megathyrae.

All the major gens of the empire had also been summoned, and their patriarchs and matriarchs had arrived and disembarked their spacecraft. Enormous royal skyliners and opulent air-barges floated in the clouds about the Mazda, each wildly different in design. Heads of twelve major gens in total were represented — summoned by Emperor Automedon.

Telesterion sat watching the proceedings from his viewport aboard his family skyliner, *The Vandal.* It was the flagship of his cousin Auric. *The Vandal* was carved from meteor-rock to resemble a great jellyfish, its stone recesses twinkling with brilliant lights. It stood out among the more austere Roman avian designs, and the even more bizarre wooden Phoenecian bark. But Auric had always been an eccentric.

No longer a boy, Telesterion was now a young adult, a Mithraic Raven and acolyte of Demi-Thoth. From his viewer he witnessed the various gens representatives, standing with their personal troops and their various flags about the great square, converging towards one another. Their fluttering symbolic flags shone in the light from two suns, one much smaller than the other.

Telesterion sat cross-legged and naked, save for a golden actor's mask, through the eye-holes of which shone his bright hazel eyes. Incense drifted from an olive-wood bowl at his side, as he grabbed a long glass hooka shaped like a griffon, and from this smoked a Martian herb medley. His pupils narrowed, and he could feel himself inside them, swimming in black milk.

Soon I will enter the God-stream. To live or die. One exists here on Megathyrae, I will find it and initiate my own Sebek-trial.

There was a loud click, followed by a yawn from behind him. He turned to the far wall, the entirety of which was a bronze zodiac-sphere, being pulled by a mechanical Mithras at its center. The wheel span one more digitus with another click, and an electronic voice recited the daily astrological forecast "Measurement 365, bear constellation around the pole star."

Telesterion closed his eyes as it spoke. *Hail Mithras, time-god. Hail to the couriers of Helios, under the protection of the sun.*

The naked slave girls Maesis and Baetis, lounging in his wicker sleep-nest beneath the zodiac, were roused by the horoscope. Telesterion watched appreciatively as the nymphs rose and lithely padded over to him. Their long hair tied up in elaborate braids, spilling out in long tendrils, their ankles and waists adorned with thin and elegant gold chains linked with serpent-heads. Their original duty had been as attendants.

"Baetis is pregnant. You have impregnated a slave." Maesis said.

Telesterion was unreadable behind his mask. "Oh? Have I?" He put his hand on Baetis' belly, still flat and smooth.

"You will marry her and she will become a noble." Maesis said.

"I cannot marry, as a mere raven of Mithras. But I will free her and the child, if that's what she wants. You as well, any time you want. It's not so easy as a freeman, though."

"She knows a union is impossible. She has done this on purpose, to raise her status." Maesis was teasing, but Baetis paid no heed whatsoever, busying herself running her hands over his shoulders.

"Our class differences would remain immutable. Have children if you want them, you will always be in my patronage."

Telesterion reached out and picked up a curved Mayana knuckle-spike, its bronze edge crisply sharp. This he slowly drew across his forearm, already criss-crossed with older scars, drawing beads of blood which dripped into an ivory plate with a Mithraic bull on its rim. He slipped off his mask, loosing long and slightly curled sandy blonde hair. He had a strong and classical nose, large eyes resting on high cheekbones. He said an ancestor's prayer before dipping his finger in the plate and placing a spot of blood on his forehead.

Maesis reached up and stroked Telesterion's sidelocks with an elegant arm, her silver serpent bracelets glinting in the blue light. He took a drop of blood and dabbed it on her head as well, as Baetis began to lick some blood from his forearm. He pointed over to where the throng was gathering. The square was dominated by a stone imperial Roman eagle, so large it was seemingly carved from a mountain of rock. Similarly there were seven natural rock structures - like towers - rising from the gigantic marble square, with small watch-towers atop each. In each of these were what looked like stick-men in long robes.

"What are they?" Maesia asked.

"Those tall things, those are men," he replied. "The seven guild leaders, at master level they are changed."

"Those are the guild masters? They look like they walk on stilts."

"They are no longer quite human." Telesterion answered nonchalantly, slowly sliding his gold mask back on. "There are seven masters because of the seven other spheres which revolve in the opposite direction to that of heaven. They are the chief masters of The Atomics and Electrics Guild, The Shipbuilders Guild, The Meteor-masons, The Geneticists, The Astrologist and Navigation guild, The Secondary Reality Masters, the Merchants and Planetary guild, and even the Thieving Guild."

"The thieves! Why?"

"I don't know all these things — but the thieving guild contains within it other unlawful guilds, I expect that as long as they are managed by a code of conduct, their influence is measurable. You'd have to ask my cousin the Magnatus."

"Magnatus Aedeseus does not answer questions from slave girls. What will the Guild Masters do?"

"They have convened on the

state of their respective arts, before the ghost of Automedon. Now they will adjudicate and record the congress of the royal families, also before the emperor." They could see the giant onyx sphinx, which housed the emperor's spirit, sitting on the plain beyond the towers. "Then with luck, we might expect Automedon's announcement."

"Which shall be what?" Baetis asked. Telesterion smiled at their world-naivety.

"How can I say?"

"Guess!"

After a pause Telesterion said: "He never actually speaks of course, his opinion shall be determined by Igoras and by augury, based on the light patterns of his trapped genius. Igoras shall then likely announce that Automedon is finally surrendering the throne to his nephew Scyles, for the reason of being dead nearly sixteen years, and go finally to his peaceful repose. Auric believes he will also announce plans for the seeding of the outer cosmos..."

"Seeding?"

"Exploring, colonizing."

"How interesting!"

"They will follow the path of the lightspear, you can see it there, a thin white line in the sky. The light emanates from the hand of Thoth in Rome, aiming outward towards a place which Thoth wishes us to migrate." *Auric believes this. They must have some new way to achieve it.*

He looked back at the wall once more, to the bronze Mithras pulling the zodiac. *Bear around the pole star.* He then turned back upon the square of shuffling nobles, and noticed a strange, sunfish-shaped vessel landing between larger corsairs. It was crudely painted with esoteric symbols.

"Jupiter!" Baetis whispered, following his gaze. "*A wytch-ship!*"

Telesterion narrowed his eyes. Baetis was the smarter of the two. "Nama patri, it is true."

"What is it, master?" Maesis

raised her head quickly, a tail of her long brown hair splayed about her naked shoulder.

"Wytch-ships ferry the faithful to Megathyrae," he said. "The Godstream initiates. As I shall be myself, one day." *If I can follow them I will find it.*

Maesis remained in rapture of the sun-fish vessel, as Baetis began kissing his neck. Telesterion sat back upon the silk cushions, but did not take his eyes from the wytch-ship, so out of place with the royal corsairs. *Auric would not welcome this sight. No. He will not want any complications to plans — already vast and rich of detail. I will find out more myself.*

"Shall we pray to Lord Mithras, to that second sun?" Baetis asked, her pretty eyebrow raised.

"Mithras is not the sun, but conquered the sun."

Maetis began to smoke from the hooka, and coughed as she spoke. "And why do they have a second sun, master?"

"A neutron-moon, a false second-sun, because we are so far from Sol."

"I did not know they could do such things."

"Nobody did." *Perhaps that is the secret to the seeding.*

"So they have a second day, an eternal day?"

"No, in fact in a few hours night will fall. Seeing as here in Pluto's orbit, a day lasts for an earth's week, our timing is fortunate..." he trailed off quietly.

"Fortunate why?" Baetis asked, but he did not answer. *I shall go down to that ship when darkness falls.*

An electronic bell sounded alerting them that Telesterion had a guest, and the girls ran to hide, as he quickly threw on his uniform, greaves and an eccentric ,beaded cloak and hood. A large floating stone head greeted him at his door, carved with beard and deep brow, like a philosopher, with large sapphires for eyes. It was his mistress Birog's Lycaodaemon, Ajaxanes. The stone contained the memory and nervous system of the legendary smithy master Ajaxenes Vitus, whose brain had survived intact where his body had not.

"Your mistress is ready, we depart now to this cursed rock." Ajaxenes said crankily, in his low electronic voice, and Telesterion followed him out, without a word. When they were gone the two nymphs rushed to the viewport again, giggling, until they saw Telesterion disembark the ship with the Ducissa's harem retinue.

Ducissa Birog, and her close confidant, Megalesia crossed the Mazda square with her harem retinue in tow: attendant slaves, nymphaeum, eunuchs, and her three young children: twin girls Esthenia and Oesal, and their two year old brother, Machaon. Birog quietly recited prayers as they went, as Megalsesis bore a bright flaming torch. Behind them her slave girls played the electric lute, and beyond them Telesterion and Ajaxenes followed at the rear.

They had awakened yesterday, after a year in cryo-sleep journeying to Pluto. She was not certain they would ever be returning home to Triton. Her husband Auric had gone on ahead of them, departing three months previously, and she was relieved they were soon to be reunited. Though Birog was now a wife to a Roman Magnatus she never discarded her Keltic roots. She remained the great beauty of her harem, effortlessly. Her abundant red hair was tied up, and her gown was translucent silk, forever fearless in her nakedness, with a gold circlet about her waist with a jewelled pendant of Cernunnos.

Her confidant Megalesia was also a great beauty, and both of them outshone their own harem-staff of young mistresses, nymphs and dancers, some of which in their bloom. All were encircled with her husband's blackly armoured, centipedal shock-centurions.

"Again Axiocersa does not attend." Birog whispered to Megalesia.

"She is growing further apart from us, and for what reason?"

"Axiocersa was not cut out for this life, she spent so much time as a slave."

"Slave? As did we? Our master kept us in luxury fit for any noble."

"She does not know what to do with herself, she has fallen to excess. I catch her making her bathing slaves have sex, while she watches. I have seen her be cruel to servants and soldiers. She is unhappy, unwell."

"She must take a husband, Ducissa."

"If needs be I shall select one for her, and that will be that. I know a gladiator who will treat her firmly."

Megalesia frowned at first, as though she found this harsh, but she could not argue with the reasoning.

"A person who cannot control themselves, requires a controller."

To their left she saw the representatives of Gens Corinth from Venus, the wealthiest family in the empire, and to her right approached Gens Leofwin, a Saxon family from Mars, who were extremely influential. The Leofwin clan were disembarking from the mouth of a giant iron herring, the bow of their Saxon skyliner. She could see the keen and sharp features of their patriarch, Saewulf, from where she stood in the shadow of the iron mouth. He stared back at her, sternly, unwaveringly, with old, wolfish eyes like piercing diamonds.

They walked on, observing at the distance the twelve royal families all slowly converging upon the inner circle of the plain, where sat the black sphinx, beneath the shadow of the gargantuan imperial eagle. Birog's path took them near the edge of the Mazda, affording an opportunity to look over the edge of the floating sky-island. She saw quick-moving clouds, so thick that the planet below could have been a gas giant, a roiling sea of vapour. The very odd break in cloud-cover revealed a bleak, rocky landscape, touched with frost, far below. There was a cold feeling bout the place, and she thought ill of it, instantly. *Nothing good will come of us being here.*

They saw the Guild Masters atop their towers, with their long, insect-like limbs and robes flowing. A calligraphus was recording the entire scene for posterity on a tablet-scroll. She stared at the sphinx and felt an ominous dread from this dark object, which seemed to absorb light instead of reflecting it.

"What will they do, the guild masters? Will they speak to us?"

"They only speak with each other. The emperor has moved them out here to Pluto's orbit, to Megathyrae, closer to him, along with the rest of us."

"Does he intend to make this desolate rock the new Rome?" Megalesia was speaking ironically, but Birog did not reply, not wishing to break her spirits. *Yes he does, sister. We may never again go home.*

A male voice intruded on their conversation. "He has brought us out to keep better tabs on us, no doubt." It was Patrician Saewulf, the Saxon. He wore a high-collared green tweed cavalry suit, and kept his silver hair shoulder length. His features were very bird-like, very observant. Flanking either side of him were his adult sons, Hereward and Ethelgar, who both stared at Megalesia, with knitted brows.

"He has us now where he wants us, Saewulf." Birog replied, smiling. Their families were allied for reasons of strategy, not blood, and she did not know could she truly trust him. Saewulf's bright azure eyes just twinkled.

"It is said among the other families, Ducissa, that your husband is now a harder man to cross than Automedon, that as the mouth of Thoth, he cannot be denied. Luckily no one doubts his tortured honesty. I scarcely think you need worry about much of anything, compared to the rest of us."

"The greater the responsibility the greater the worry. But my husband has no designs on being emperor, you can rest assured, Saewulf."

"I rest most assuredly knowing I remain in your good graces, Ducissa. The currents of power are rarely in truth what they appear on the surface. The fact remains he would be the *best* emperor — and precisely because as Thoth's interpreter he has both the power to be and because he does not wish to be."

She was disquieted by his candid talk, and could not determine his goal. *How could he speak so brazenly, here, in the shadow of Automedon?* "The demi-god Thoth may have no real interest in politics, or immediate affairs," she managed.

He looked to Telesterion beyond her. "I knew the boy's father, Oedimon, well. A great man. I wish nothing but the best for your family, sincerely." The older Saxon gave a brief but unmistakable look of genuine concern at this, and nodded as he walked on. She felt an instant softening towards him.

They came to their position on the square, facing the other families. The massive imperial eagle cast a long shadow across the marble plain, making the large sphinx look like a toy. All the soldiers accompanying each gens took up a formation surrounding their nobility. Immediately Birog spotted across the divide the gold mask and long ornate Keltic kafkan of Euergetes Rex of Neptune, surrounded by his tattooed keterna. Between the soldiers and him was a gaggle of fashionably dressed concubines and wives.

"He pretends not to see us," Megalesia said.

"I am glad of it."

"They say Euergetes has become a religiously pious man and repentant of his former sins."

Birog snorted a laugh at this, and Megalesia continued: "Auric and Automedon should have had him removed."

"It is his alliance with Automedon which saves him, not my husband."

Megalesia sneered "Those hens who follow him, born wealthy, see them stare at us. Prostitutes and crones. He carries himself like an oriental despot. He is nobody now."

Birog looked all about. She recognized all the great heads, some ancient enemies. The Ouranians, Martians, Venusians, Saturnalians, Mercurians, the great tribes of Jupiter, Greco-Egyptian, Mayana-Ostrogoth, the elongated heads of the strange Scythian's of Io, now a powerful merchant clan. Certain religious leaders were present, but only the very elite. She saw amongst the throng the War Pontifex of Ares-Mars, a master druid hidden in a hood, and Caracallus the chief sky-priest of the temple of Jupiter.

Directly across the square from her stood the patriarch of the Hyksos gens, a heavily armoured man of long white beard carrying a staff.

"Who is that?" Megalesia asked.

"Gehethen. It is said he is controversially a convert to a new variant cult of Christianity, and violently opposed to the god-stream."

The throng was loudly muttering among each other and themselves, amid the distant sound of wind and the strange silent observance of the guild masters above them.

"What will happen? What will become of us in this place?" Megalesia asked, but Birog had no answer. She sorely wished Auric was with them.

But where was he?

She turned and motioned for Ajaxenes and Telesterion to move up and stand by her side. They could see worry in her eyes. Finally over the noise came a single loud voice, it was Gehethen, who yelled daringly:

"What are we doing here?"

"Where is Igoras?" Joined Saewulf the Saxon.

The crowd became silent, so that there was for a moment only the sound of the wind, then very slowly a golden holoplasm appeared, at a magnitude Birog had never seen or dreamed possible. It was of Igoras, unmistakable in his neat uniform and immaculately combed, thinning hair. The holoplasm was so gargantuan it was as though he stood outside the Mazda, on the surface of the planet, and only his head and shoulders could be seen over the edge of their floating island, like a gigantomachy demi-god holding up a stone. His voice came loud and booming across the square.

"Welcome, mighty gens of the undying solar empire. Welcome to Megathyrae. Welcome to New Rome."

"Igoras!" Many cried aloud, some jubilantly, some angrily, depending. Some, she thought, sounded fearful.

"And where is Automedon?" Gehethen exclaimed boldly, raising his staff high.

"He is here," the Igoras holoplasm said, in barely a whisper, which was still very loud, and his giant hand gestured to the sphinx.

"Silent in death, as usual, with only you to interpret." *Gehethen was very bold,* Birog thought. *Too bold.*

"But I am not even here... myself." The giant holoplasm smiled, offering no explanation. The wind seemed to get stronger, howling eerily amid the crannies of the imperial eagle.

"Why are we here, what would you have of us. We cannot refuse you." Birog said at last, commandingly. "Why are you yourself not here, when we have all travelled so far? We are not mere emissaries, we are the heads of our bloodlines!"

"And what is this New Rome?" Saewulf joined with her.

Igoras laid his giant holo-hand down on the square, and within it was another, normal sized holo-plasm of himself, and the giant suddenly faded. The human-sized projection paced on the plain before the onyx sphinx, dressed in sober philosopher's robes overtop his uniform, presenting himself like a classic orator.

"I cannot be here in person as I am myself no longer strictly alive. It is easier for me to present to you this way, than as what I have become. Everyone of importance is present, there is no longer any Senatus Romanus, you assembled here represent the dissemination of the commands of your emperor, and are responsible for all those satrapies and city-states which live in your orbits. History has condensed to this moment, and there is nobody more important in the universe than all of us assembled here."

"Demi-Thoth is not here." Said Telesterion boldly, and Birog gasped with shock.

Igoras did not cease smiling. "Of course," was his only response.

"Igoras, you are not emperor." Decimus said.

"Am I not?"

There was a loud rumble of disagreement at this, even alarm. Birog's armed men became more alert. In response Euergetes' Keterna did the same across the square.

"No, of course not. But this *is* New Rome, families of the empire, rest assured. Everything is new from here on. I am not emperor, yet in some small way, I am "

"We have no reason to listen to you, or trust whatever bargains you've made with outside forces!"

Igoras only smiled, like a fox.

"Automedon is dead fifteen years!" Yelled the Greco-Egyptian gens leader Ata-Soter. "Scyles is rightful emperor now."

"The mouth of Thoth, Magnatus Auric Aedeseus should be emperor!" Yelled Saewulf, boldly, drawing his intricate Saxon sword. Birog was taken aback, then Telesterion beside her cheered, and drew his own dagger. Her troops made a formation, doubtfully training their weapons at all potentially hostile targets. Birog looked up to the Guild Masters, observing all above them like vultures. Absorbing, recording. *Who was really in charge here?*

"You put the guilds above the great families, we are the bloodlines of history!" She yelled.

Igoras the fox only smiled, and waited, until there was little but the sound of the wind once more. "The guilds protect us from the rise of mercantilism. From the ahistorical, the areligious control of pure money. The wealth..." here the holo-Igoras nodded towards the Venusians, "of many families becomes a threat to sacred Roman order, it is the artistic standard of the guilds, which must take some pre-eminence even over the noble families, as a matter of practicality."

Here Igoras faded and reappeared riding a majestic stallion, which slowly clopped todards the far tip of the shadow of the eagle.

"My friends. I understand your claims, your desires. Many of you are not what you seem, and wish for the opposite of what you say. Many mean what they say, but will achieve the opposite result. Everything is ultimately its opposite. But New Rome is already established. I shall erect monuments to Romulus and Remus on every world we build. The keystone summit-world of this project shall have a colossus of Aeneas, an onyx equestrian sculpture, the largest ever seen. Megathyrae may be crude, by your standards, but each of your kingdoms are about to expand, tenfold." Igoras' holoplasm vanished and was replaced by an animation of the solar system. They saw then many more planets being added outside the usual orbits, in an outreaching path, leading away from the sun. The path followed a line of light she guessed must be the lightspear.

Then a large projection of Igoras' head re-appeared. "A trail of new worlds has begun construction. Our fleets work at this tirelessly. My backers work at this, as does your Emperor. New planets, compacted from asteroids. The innovation developed here, the neutron-moon, shall facilitate each of these planets with their own false-sun. This will create warm and inviting worlds, infinite in number, they will be lush with life. New trading empires, economic growth. From here, we expand outwards, and make what we need as we go. And Automedon shall be your Emperor, until such time as he decides not to be."

"He is a shade. He has no connection to this plane. The dead cannot guide a living empire."

Said Gehethen.

"And why not?"

"We need proof! Proof that he is still with us, and that it is not just you. You and your hidden bargains and backers! How do we know that Automedon's shade still exists?"

"He is here." Igoras said simply, still smiling. "Behold."

From the front chest of the sphinx two panels, their edges formerly unseen, suddenly opened with a metallic clang, and a black obsidian throne hovered out of this new aperture. Seated upon the throne sat a human-like figure, about five times normal size, dressed completely in crumpled black leather, which shone in the light cast by the false second sun of Megathyrae. None of his flesh was visible, his face was a cyclopean single eye, which glowed with purple and blue light, with tubes at the mouth which ran into a panel at his chest. This thing did not move as the throne drifted out. Birog gasped with horror.

"Bow before your emperor." Igoras said, still smiling, and Birog noted Euergetes and a few others bowing.

"Automedon has transcended the barrier between the living and the dead. Between Hades and Elysium. He did not wish to relinquish this empire that he built, not now at the summit of its greatest enterprise. The breaking of the barrier to deep space. I, his handler, sensed his anguish. I offered to let him possess me, so that he might live again. And when this was done, I entered the godstream. I became a bridge for him, between this barrier. My body died, but Automedon's became once more a true force upon this material plane."

Birog could see behind the cyclopean eye a kind of mist flowing inside the leather suit. *Is he incorporeal?*

"Your emperor undertook the Sebek trial. His ghost entered the godstream. He emerged from this, something entirely new. Something.... more permanent."

Permanent, Birog thought, struggling with disbelief. *As in eternal?*

There were shocked gasps, and some cried out as the leathery black head turned this way and that, as though examining the throng of nobles for the first time.

"But he is dead?" Gehethen the Christian asked, "a Sebek trial for a ghost? A non-living god of death? This is blasphemy."

"Nooooo..." came a ghastly voice, emanating from all around them. Deep and whispery, icily inhuman. And Automedon raised his black gauntleted hand, and Gehethen's face froze in a horrific death-mask, and he dropped his staff. His armour began to crumple, and his body floated up into the air, as his flesh began to dry out, and be became both crushed and mummified before their eyes. He crumpled in upon himself in the air as Automedon's raised hand quivered.

Birog's troops had their weapons trained, awaiting her orders. There was a sense of panic. *I am alone without Auric, but I am smart enough not to start anything here.*

The fast moving clouds were suddenly glowing pink as the sky took a reddish hue in a sudden dusk. But Birog felt unsure as all the shadows turned crimson.

Is he doing that? Can he do that?

The awful ghostly voice washed over them once more, hissing slowly:

"I live.... once more."

She closed her eyes, tightly.

Later that evening, each family was led to a safehouse, where they would be informed on the details of their new outer kingdoms. No new challenges had been raised, and the strange new body of the Emperor had retreated back within the sphinx, though the crumpled corpse of Gehethen remained hovering in the air by an unknown science, on display. Telesterion had retreated, alone, to their flagship, *The Vandal,* meditating on the events which had transpired, and yet determined to investigate the wytch-ship.

Robed and hooded, he disembarked the jellyfish skyliner once more. Night had fallen on Megathyrae, though the dark sky was still somewhat bright from the distant lightspear. It cast long and crisp shadows across the smooth plain of Mazda, as Telesterion silently marched across this and past the Wytch-ship, before pausing in the shadow of an outcropping of monolith rock near the edge of the square. There were a few centurions about but they paid him little mind, many were mounting giant saddled war-birds, and taking off to patrol the clouds. There was no longer anything requiring major security. The guild masters were gone, the noble families were all in their bunkers or headed for their new homes in floating plains and hovering outcrops of land about the atmosphere of Megathyrae. All but the gens Aedeseus, Telesterion's family, those of Ata-Soter, and of the Martian Saxon, Saewulf.

The lights in the towers were out, and he hid behind the outcropping in the long shadow of a guild tower. He determined to wait there, studying the wytch-ship, from which no one had yet disembarked. He had paid off a centurion for information, and was told at night the new acolytes would be led out, to say prayers before the black sphinx, and then led to a place of waiting, which the centurion did not know or would not say.

Soon there was the hydraulic sound of a ship's ramp lowering. Staying hidden in the shadow, Telesterion peeked out to observe a procession of figures in shabby robes and animal furs, tied together in a chain at the neck, being led out of the mouth of the wytch-ship by a large slaver in a fierce gold lion-head helmet. The acolytes did indeed resemble ill-kept slaves, and were even staggering from apparent weakness. *Perhaps a holy fast is required before testing their souls in the stream?*

To his dismay a custodia of a type he had never seen, with leather armour covered all over with spikes, including his faceless helmet, and long sword of northman's type at his back, came out behind the procession and headed directly for him.

I must have been spotted.

But clever Telesterion had cunning of an unusual sort. One of the rare artifacts he had inherited from his deceased father Oedimon was his eccentric cloak, which had been described to him as 'an Octopus Cloak'. This garment adopted the exact colour and detail of whatever surrounding it found itself in: perfect camouflage.

The enormous guard came directly up to his position — but despite having detected motion, he could see nothing but shadowed rocks. The custodia's helmet turned about, perplexed, and he drew his long sword, and Telesterion had to check that he wasn't casting a visible shadow, or that anything was out of place. The cloak was not infallible to detection, and at its fringes a distortion could be seen, or a shadow momentarily cast.

After a brief but agonizing pause, the custodia retreated.

Telesterion gathered his courage about him, determining to find out more, and followed the guard back aboard the wytchship.

Inside it was dark and archaic, even rusted like an old shipping freighter. There were many dark corners and vents of steam and conjoining, zigzagging metal-mesh ramps. Telesterion followed the custodia up a gang plank overlooking an engine bay. The custodia stopped at one point, frozen for several seconds, before slowly turning his helmet around.

He is clever, he senses something, but cannot be sure.

Telesterion did not move, not even breathe, mere cubits apart from the hulking armed man. Despite his instinct, the guard eventually turned and resumed his march to the ship's cabin, and Telesterion followed, walking as silently as he could.

Looking down through the ramp grate he saw some dishevelled, dusky-looking slaves, possibly helots, working exhaustively on the engineering. The heat was oppressive and some of the equipment seemed quite alien, not a style his clan, gens Aedeseus, was famiiar with.

The royal gens have been living so distant and isolated even their technology has diverged evolutionarily. We might as well be different species at this point.

The Wytch ships came from Jupiter's moon Ganymede, home of gens Hyksos, who had been close to the family of Caesar Automedon, but Telesterion had heard rumours they were now supporters of the upstart Scyles. Despite the supposed impartiality of Thoth cult acolytes, there was a political significance to this. He dwelled upon this now, as he crept through the heart of their ship like an unwanted ghost.

He followed the guard to the end of the plank, and a very thick round iron door, like that of a vault, swung open on a sensor. Telesterion felt a tingling warning to hold back, mild sensations of psychic awareness he often experienced since he had begun experimenting with sporefumes. He was not surprised then when the guard drew his sword and took a swipe through the air behind him. Had Telesterion not paused he would have been beheaded.

The guard's face was unseen behind the helmet, but Telesterion could sense he was chuckling now at his own paranoia, as he sheathed his sword and stepped through the door. Telesterion paused once more, in doubt this time, and just for a moment, before following him through. The door shut behind him.

Inside was an oval iron chamber, and at its center was a ragged but lusty Egyptian woman in a traditional curled wig attending to what appeared to be a fat and oily Hyksos man shorn completely of hair. The man looked squalid and tough, and Telesterion noted with some alarm that he kept a dog near his seat. But the animal only looked at him with a mild curiosity, sniffing the air, and not barking. The woman cooed and fussed over this brute as he spoke to a low-quality holoplasm of another man's head. The head was a monochrome red hue and fuzzy, but Telesterion made out a curled beard and solemn Roman face. The spiked custodia stood to attention near the door.

"Everything has been done as instructed," the Hyksos was assuring the holoplasm, mumbling as he chewed dates the woman brought him. "We have deposited our human cargo. Those poor wretches. I have heard nothing about the activities of assassin guilds or gens patriarchs replaced with aufs. All is quiet on this godless gehenna-rock, in fact the idea that something exciting might even accidentally happen is quite impossible. My life is wasted now, a pawn in larger games, left to rot at the limits of humanity. There is nothing out here at all, DemiGaius, though you can speak comfortably from your villa in Rome."

Auf! Telesterion thought, *the gothic term for duplici — a doppelganger! Replacing gens patriarchs? And DemiGaius, I know that name? What in Jupiter's name are these Hyksos up to?*

"Zyke you fat coward. You greasy garum-merchant. Do not mention these things on open channels. Just report when anything does happen. It shouldn't take too long."

Telesterion saw a small symbol, a holoplasm marker beneath DemiGaius' disembodied head. It was an emerald ring. *Automedon's gens — Princeps Scyles!*

The Hyksos man made a pleading gesture with his hands as he smiled grimly, his teeth dirty with dates. "Please, master, allow me some humour. It's all I have in this place, so far from the sun, so cold and isolated. I am colder and more lost than that Magnatus..."

The holoplasm snorted a derisive laugh. "You cannot follow even the most basic command or security protocol, I'm ending transmission."

Magnatus! Something has happened to Auric!

When the holoplasm had flickered out the Hyksos spat. "DemiGaius! I am a simple freight captain, I know nothing of your plans and I wish to know less — bastard!"

Suddenly the vault door opened and the woman went through.

I am witnessing a plot and

must get word to the others.

At that Telesterion took his chance, and ran quickly back out the door before it shut. He passed near to the spiked custodia, who seemed to look towards him, or sense him somehow once more. But too late, as Telesterion was out, and raced back the way he had come, unseen.

Birog was at last reunited with her husband.

They had retired solemnly to their new temporary residence, an impressive white-lime cave structure within the heart of the citadel. It was a hive-like network of curved, organic rock formations and curated mining bores, linking and looping in successive cave-chambers, about a central gens planning room, where she now convened. Her harem had been dismissed, except for Ajaxenes, Megalesia, and her eunuch Meges. She finally met with Auric in their private quarters, a vast elliptical cave, lush with plants and growing grape vines, with small rivulets of natural meteor-water, amethyst in colour, trickling about smooth, white, snaking stone tributaries in the walls and floors.

She saw Auric for the first time dismissing most of his retinue of his centurions, at the far end of their domicile. His long blonde hair in plaits, as usual, his heavy and richly detailed robes of office overtop his leather segmented armour. The stone head of Ajaxenes, forever her council, had arrived ahead of her, and now floated over.

"Mistress," Ajaxenes said in his echoey artifical voice, "it is my opinion that something here is slightly wrong, specifically in the behaviour of your husband, whom I have noticed in the past to be nothing but warm and affectionate towards his family, who he places as priority, above all else. But who seems now unsually aloof."

Birog was frozen with horror to hear this. She suppressed an immediate rage towards Ajaxenes, to interfere with their overdue and private reunion this way, before thinking calmly again, regally, with a view to their surroundings.

Surrounded by enemies, she thought.

"I Understand. I'm sure my husband is laboured by extreme burdens of decison-making and responsibility at this present moment, and we must allow him some room for distraction. Even regarding his family."

Ajaxenes said nothing, but did not leave her side as Auric made his way towards them, stepping over the little glittering mauve streams, smiling with his arms outstretched. Her throat constricted with sudden worry and terror.

In his approach now, his movements seem foreign. But this is madness, I am paranoid!

They embraced at last, beneath a shining oval oculus in the center room, from which poured out an artificial but warm golden light, as the neutron-moon had set.

Birog knew instantly that something was in fact wrong. He kissed her, but somewhat nervously, and looking into his eyes she saw nothing. She saw even something like trepidation, unease. Too soon, he backed away from her. "I must go now to my somatophylax, and we must meet with the saxon Saewulf and the emmissaries of Igoras."

Birog gave him a worried look, holding his arm, her eyes imploring. "My love, if you have any secrets burdening you, anything you want to tell me, now is the..."

"No, I cannot impart anything else to you now. Please be strong. Take care of the children." He backed away from her, still smiling. Even this was not like something he would say. She could not place what it was exactly that was wrong, or what it was she saw in that smile. But it was something akin to culpability, even a mild fear. Like he had committed some evil and was at risk of being noticed.

It's not that he isn't in his right mind — It simply is not like him in any way, apart from appearance. But if it is not — then where is he? She felt incredible confusion and rising fear.

As Auric turned to leave, and his centurions with him, suddenly the air before her began to shimmer and vibrate, until something tore a rent in reality, to reveal Telesterion, standing before her. He had a curved dagger drawn in one hand, and with the other he pressed a finger to his lips, suggesting her silence, as she stood in speechless amazement.

Then he drew his camouflage cloak back about him, and turned to follow Auric from the cave.

TO BE CONTINUED...

Well, there are certainly a lot of events and characters in this unfolding future Roman timeline. You may need to work hard to keep track of it all. Take notes or something.

There is great dramatic potential, Ramek thinks, in such a timeline, which occurs outside Ramek's, although he can visit in in stories, like you do.

Who will wind up true emperor of the Solar Empire? Auric? Scyles? Or will it be Automedon.... forever?

Well that inevitable hour has come to pass, kiddies, the October issue draws to a close. Have a scary Halloween, and remember to watch for patterns in the system. Keep your firesords blazing...

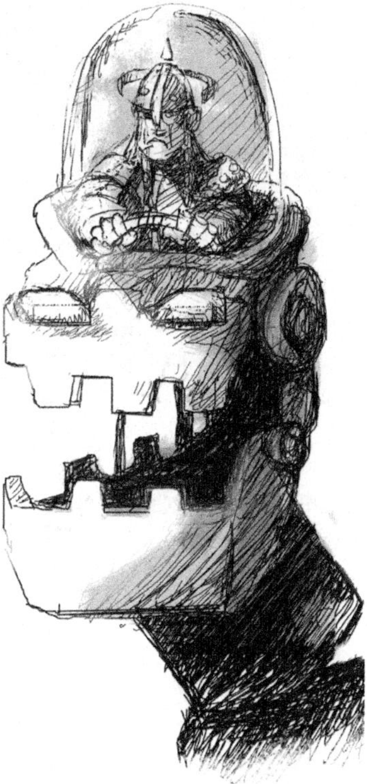

Mailbag: Dear Ramek

MAILBAG:

Dear Ramek,
I am a rare girl fan! I thought your depictions in issue 2 were very sexy and dangerous. Can you be drawn in more romantic scenarios?

XOXOXO
CYNDI SMALLPOX
New Jersey, USA

Thank you Cyndi.
Ramek cannot do romantic posing for a publication such as Aegeon, but might be available at a private price. Ramek will romance you by throwing you on his saddlebags and taking to the air on his warbird. Many nymphs and scrogs have been similarly romanced, terrified with fright above the clouds.

Dear Sirs,
Why does Aegeon not stick to a particular type of sci-fi? It even has horror and fantasy in it. It's not even strictly pulp. What is it?

Regards,
CIARAN
Galway, Ireland

Dear Ramek...

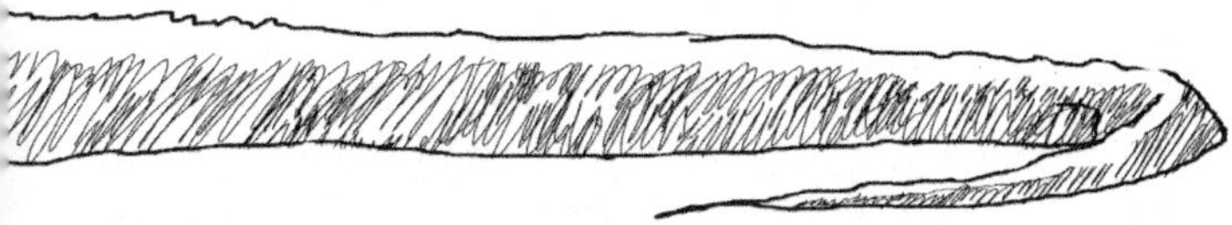

Ciaran. Do not whine, like a bleating, hapless sea cucumber, because your solid gold entertainment is eccentric and not precisely like some variant you are more accustomed to. I will grate you like cheese if this whining appears before me once more! Aegeon is whatever it wants to be. I don't think you will find anything too upsettingly surprising in any issue.

Ramek the Machine-Slayer,
Will 'Ferrand', ' I am Dreaming', 'Patriarch', 'Onyx Horseman', and the other serials appear in every issue from here on? WIll these later be published as novels?

RANDALL STEWART
British Columbia, Canada

Not every issue, they willl appear as needed, or as written, until they are all written. Then indeed, they may appear as full tomes as Aureus Press publications, or independent. Dune itself appeared intially in serial format (in Analog Magazine, Ramek believes). It is a good way to play out a potential novel, crafted in mini-cliffhangers, which is precisely the type of classic storytelling Ramek and the crew of Aegeon and the submitting authors are here to deliver and encourage.

Ramek,
are the ladies more desirous of you after having some machine parts. or are they repulsed?

RON
Telegram question

Ron,
Attraction is of no consequence. It is not possible to refuse Ramek.

Editors of Aegeon,
What is your opinion of the current state of imaginative fiction? I mean in the mainstream?

DENNIS MEDIEROS
Brasil

Ramek can speak for everyone involved with Aegeon in say ing the state of this long-standing craft, like so many others, is quite abysmal. Even outside this specific genre, the 'mainstream' itself has almost nothing of cultural value in it any longer - anywhere. Let alone thought-provoking ideas like those found in Aegeon, which hurt and confuse the brain of the postmodern human livestock of your age. It seems culture of your time is make-up tutorials, cute cat videos, and anime pornography.

All the classic era publishers of fantasy and science fiction are now signalling-depots for social justice, like most mainstream things. Sadly many of these classic titles still exist, though their natural fan base is not even aware of this, as they exist now only to insult their fanbase and fail at everything. Even worse than valueless, I would say, they are producing anti-work, that is work which is beyond poor or moribund, but actively attacks and denigrates their chosen art, mocking and belittling all their own former glories.

Like George Lucas and the surviving members of Metallica, they seem to not understand what it was that made them great to begin with.

There are of course other independent publishers, (like Aegeon) thanks largely to the better aspects of the internet. Some of these other publications we have a close association, with (such as Bizarchives and Toadstoolmag). Others, Ramek is sure, will soon be emerging on the market as well. The old guard have failed, and have become senile, and must become the compost upon which the new seeds shall sprout.
- Ramek

Dear Ramek,
Will you appear once more in Aegeon - not as host and narrator, but in a story piece? Hails and greetings from Sweden!

ERIC
Malmö

This is entirely possible, Eric, considering Ramek never ceases having adventures, and has a yarn for every day of the week. Both truthful and not-so-truthful.

Perhaps even the next issue, will contain such a wonderful and heart-racing tale.

That about wraps it up for Issue Three, scroats. Agrathrag, and goodbye, Sign up for our mailing list and make sure you don't miss the next issue.

www.aegeon-scifi.com/ subscriptions/

Printed in Great Britain
by Amazon

23148557R00104